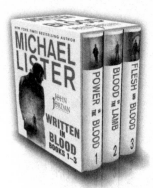
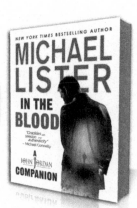

Also by Michael Lister

Inquiries should be addressed to:
Pulpwood Press
P.O. Box 35038
Panama City, FL 32412

Lister, Michael.
Cold Blood / Michael
Lister.
-----1st ed.
p. cm.

ISBN: 978-1-888146-72-1 Paperback
ISBN: 978-1-888146-71-4 Hardcover

Book Design and Production: Novel Design Studio
www.noveldesignstudio.com

Printed in the United States

1 3 5 7 9 10 8 6 4 2

First Edition

COLD BLOOD

A

JOHN JORDAN

MYSTERY | BOOK THIRTEEN

MICHAEL LISTER

PULPWOOD PRESS
PANAMA CITY, FL

Dedication

For Tim Flanagan

You are such a tremendous gift to me and John, and a true partner in these crimes. Thank you for treating these books as if they were your own. You have gone above and beyond in every way on every project, and for the first time in my twenty-year career I'm happy for readers to judge my books by their covers. Thank you, thank you, thank you!

Thank Yous

For doing and giving and supporting and helping so much, thank you, Dawn Lister, Jill Mueller, Aaron Bearden, Micah Lister, Sheriff Mike Harrison, Judge Terry Lewis, Dr. D.P. Lyle, and Tim Flanagan of Novel Design Studio.

That Night

It had rained earlier in the evening and the damp pavement shimmers in the headlights.

Raindrops fall intermittently from the pines lining the road, thudding wetly on the moist earth below.

The quiet night is cloud-shrouded, the desolate coastal highway dark, and the foggy air thick with moisture as particles of water dance in the cylindrical shafts of light.

She is driving far faster than she should.

She wonders why. Why is she being so careless, so reckless? Does her life really matter so little to her? Is this a death wish or something else? An attempt at numbing the numbness? A test of the invincibility she feels?

Something in the road.

Brake. Turn. Avoid.

A gray fox darts out of the sand pine scrub and onto the highway, its long tail trailing behind it.

The speeding car swerves to miss it—and does, but hits a patch of standing water and begins to hydroplane.

Spinning. Sliding. Skidding.

The car slams into a guardrail then careens off it back onto the road, spins again, then comes to rest facing the opposite direction on the other side of the road.

Moments pass.

Then minutes.

She climbs out of the car, not particularly shaken, stands and surveys the damage.

Steam rises from the hot hood of the car. Wipers rub across the mostly dry windshield.

Then from out of the dark, diffused by the fog, approaching headlights appear in the distance, glowing eerily in the mist.

From the *In Search of Randa Raffield* podcast intro:

On Thursday, January 20, 2005, the day of George W. Bush's second inauguration, twenty-one-year-old Randa Raffield crashed her car on a secluded stretch of Highway 98 near the Gulf of Mexico, not far from Port St. Joe.

Randa was a student-athlete at the University of West Florida in Pensacola, a champion swimmer. She was five feet seven inches tall with dark auburn-tinted hair, pale white skin, and large green eyes.

Nineteen days before, at a little after midnight on New Year's Eve, Randa's boyfriend, Josh Douglas, proposed to her at the Pensacola Pelican Drop, the New Year's Eve event in downtown Pensacola. She said yes. The proposal was captured by both local TV news stations and attendees with their cellphones, and has now been shared millions of times online.

The location of the wreck was hundreds of miles from where she was supposed to be.

She was on the phone with her mom at the time.

Moments after the accident, Roger Lamott, a truck driver hauling fuel, came upon the scene. Randa refused his help, asked him not to call the police, and said she preferred to wait alone for the towing service she had already called.

After pulling away, Lamott called the police anyway.

It was later discovered that Randa hadn't called the police or a towing service and her car was drivable.

Both her mom and Roger Lamott gave statements indicating Randa wasn't injured or particularly upset by the incident.

Seven minutes later when the first Gulf County Sheriff's Deputy arrived, Randa was gone, vanished without a trace.

She was never seen again.

Chapter One

"I know you've worked a lot of baffling cases," Merrick says, "but I guarantee you've never seen anything like this."

Merrick McKnight and I are sitting on the deck at the Dockside Café on the marina in Port St. Joe on a warm September day, waiting for our lunch to arrive. The marina is just across the way from where St. Joe Paper Company's old paper mill used to stand, but all that remains of it now is the lasting environmental damage it did.

We're here to talk about the possibility of me helping with his investigation into the Randa Raffield case.

"Tell me," I say.

"What's that phrase . . . It's a riddle wrapped in a mystery inside an enigma."

"Russia," I say.

"Huh?"

"It's what Churchill said about Russia."

"Well, he could've been talking about this case. It's the same thing. Every time I think I have a handle on it, I learn something else or learn that the thing I thought I had learned a while back was wrong. It keeps changing, keeps turning and twisting. It's all blind alleyways and dead-end streets."

I nod. Nearly every case feels like that at some point or another. But from the little I know about the disappearance of Randa Raffield, it might be even more like that than others.

"And this whole thing's exploding," he says. "Gotten way out of control."

"The investigation? Your podcast? What?"

He nods. "Both. Everything. It's all blown up in ways we never could've imagined . . . and we really need your help."

Some six months ago, he and Daniel Davis began a true crime podcast to investigate the disappearance of Randa Raffield.

Merrick is a reporter and the partner of Reggie Summers, the sheriff of Gulf County and my boss. Daniel is a retired religion professor and the husband of Sam Michaels, an FDLE agent I worked a case with back in the spring. Though I know their partners far better, I like and respect both men—and think they're particularly good at podcasting.

"When we started we had no idea what it would become," he says. "What it would stir up, or how many crazies it'd cause to crawl out of their holes."

"Reggie mentioned how well the show's doing," I say.

Though true crime has long been a popular genre for books and documentaries, its popularity has exploded in the age of new media. Beginning with Sarah Koenig's podcast *Serial* and continuing with Netflix's *Making a Murderer*, HBO's documentary miniseries *The Jinx*, and Sundance's series *The Staircase*, true crime content is experiencing a renaissance and gaining a following unlike anything since *In Cold Blood*, *Helter Skelter*, and *The Thin Blue Line.*

A young woman with skin tanned bronze in short shorts and a pink Dockside T-shirt delivers our grouper baskets and we begin to eat.

The day is bright and clear, the bay behind the marina peaceful and picturesque, and the bay breeze the gulls and swallow-tailed kites glide on and that blows through the open restaurant has just a hint of fall in it.

Tim Munn, the manager, stops by the table to check on us and to give us samples of a special gumbo he's been working on with the kitchen.

Merrick samples the gumbo before I do and gushes over it to such a degree that I give him mine.

As Tim moves on to hand out samples to other customers, a massive yacht slowly eases into the marina.

"What do you attribute the show's popularity to?" I ask. "Both with the general public and to deranged internet trolls."

"I think we do a decent job with our production, but it's the case itself that compels people. The mystery is so . . . maddening. There are so many clues, so many possibilities, and the window of opportunity for something to happen to her was so small. Less than seven minutes for her to vanish off the face of the earth—and stay that way for nearly twelve years now. Plus she was so pretty and popular and . . . It's easy to get obsessed with it. Daniel and I have gone to some pretty dark places, jumped down more than a few rabbit holes. But we're not just popular. We're controversial too. We've made mistakes."

"Mistakes are part of investigating," I say. "Sometimes the biggest part."

"It's given me a greater appreciation for what you and Reggie do. Especially you. She says you're the best investigator she's ever worked with."

It's nice of her to say, nice of him to share, but Reggie has worked with very few investigators over the course of her short career in law enforcement.

"Does she know you're talkin' to me about this?" I ask.

He nods. "When I told her I'd be asking for your help with it, she said she knew you'd talk to her about it no matter what you decided."

I nod. "I will. It'll be her call, but if we get involved it'll be officially. It's an unsolved case in our jurisdiction."

"You couldn't just help me and Daniel a little?" he says. "Unofficially."

I shake my head. "Not as long as I'm working for the sheriff's department."

"We're really close. I think. I've thought that before, but . . . we've uncovered so much information. I know the answer is in there. We just need help putting the pieces together the right way."

I nod and look out over the bay again to see a gull gliding just above the surface of the water.

"I thought my career was over," Merrick says. "As a reporter. As an investigative journalist. This podcast has given me a second chance . . . and it's been even better for Daniel. I think it's kept him from going crazy during all this with Sam. He can do it all from home while he takes care of her—but it gives him something to do, keeps his mind occupied. But this isn't about us. It's about Randa. Finding out what the hell happened to her. That's why I'm asking for your help. Our podcast is a success and I've got interest in my book."

"I didn't know you were working on a book."

"That's how it all started. My point is we'll be fine. If it gets solved, we'll finish the book and start a new season of the podcast investigating another unsolved case. If it doesn't, we'll keep working on this one. We'll be fine either way. My main motive here is to get justice for Randa."

"I don't doubt that, but just to show good faith, what are some of your non-main-motives?"

He smiles. "Well, let's see. We need help. A fresh set of eyes on this thing. We've hit a wall. Not sure how much further we can take it without . . . And like I said . . . it's blowing up. We're gettin' a lot of attention. Not all of it good. We got crazies and scaries crawling out of the computer. We're losing control of it."

"It?"

"The . . . case, I guess. The investigation. But mostly the discussion about it. The circus surrounding it. And . . . if I'm being completely transparent . . . we now have some competition. Our biggest critic has started his own podcast about the case and says he's working on a book too."

I nod. "Thank you for being so honest."

"I meant what I said. I just want it solved. Truth is, all I want is for you to look into it. If you do, you won't be able to help yourself. It's too mysterious, too maddening. You'll investigate it. And if you do, we'll solve it. I know it."

Chapter Two

When I leave Dockside, I head west on Highway 98 toward the spot where Randa's car was found, listening to Merrick and Daniel's podcast as I do.

"Welcome to another edition of *In Search of Randa Raffield*," Merrick says. "I'm your host, Merrick McKnight, and I'm joined as always by Daniel Davis. Hey Daniel. You ready for another exciting episode today?"

"I am."

I cross over the small bridge between the sites where the paper mill and chemical plant used to be and then over the much larger George G. Tapper Bridge above the Gulf County Canal that connects the Intracoastal Waterway with St. Joseph Bay, the bay extending out to the left beneath me, the sun refracting off the surface of the water causing me to squint. Coming down off the bridge into Highland View, I put on my shades.

"Well, let's get right to it," Merrick says.

He is the more natural podcaster of the two—more relaxed and comfortable, his voice deeper and richer—but I know from listening to a few of the other shows that Daniel contributes a lot, and the two men work well together.

"Today we're going to focus on the location where Randa went missing," Merrick says. "But before we do that, let's do a quick review for everyone—especially first-time listeners."

"Sure," Daniel says. "On Thursday, January 20, 2005, Randa Raffield, a twenty-one-year-old student at the University of West Florida, crashed her car on a secluded stretch of Highway 98, between Mexico Beach and Port St. Joe, Florida."

I am driving along that very spot right now, coming up on the Dixie Belle Motel on my left and, farther down, Barefoot Cottages on my right, and it's a bit disconcerting to be hearing them talk about it as I do.

The Dixie Belle Motel is a 1950s-style roadside motor lodge. Barefoot Cottages is a gated community of coastal cottages—residents and rentals. Both of these developments, combined with Windmark Beach beyond, starkly contrast the rundown, empty, and abandoned buildings lining the highway just a short way back in Highland View. It's at intersections like these that impoverished Old Florida fishing villages clash with the New Florida exclusive developments and pristine master-planned communities that are the vacation destinations and second homes for the wealthy of Atlanta and Birmingham.

"She was supposed to be at an Iraq war protest in Atlanta that coincided with the second George W. Bush inauguration," Daniel continues, "so the place where she wrecked was over three-hundred miles from where she was supposed to be. All her friends and family had no idea she wasn't in Atlanta—even her mom who she was on the phone with at the time of the accident—"

Merrick breaks in. "And we should say that all her friends and family and even her boyfriend claim they thought she was in Atlanta, based on the statements they've made, but we haven't interviewed all of them yet. We hope to. We're trying to."

"Right," Daniel says. "We're reporting what's out there—in statements and news stories and interviews—then asking our own questions and doing our own investigation. Right now we're just recapping. So she wrecks her car near the new-at-the-time Windmark Beach subdivision. From all accounts she is okay, not injured or even really upset. Not long after the accident—how long we can't be completely sure about—a truck driver pulls up, rolls down his window, and asks if she's okay. She is out of the car, standing near it."

I pull up and park on the side of the highway just down from the entrance to Windmark in the exact spot where Randa's abandoned car had been found.

"The truck driver's name is Roger Lamott," Merrick says.

"Yes. According to Lamott, Randa was fine and didn't want his help. Didn't want him calling the police. Didn't want him calling a tow truck. Didn't want him giving her a ride or waiting with her. We don't know if she had been drinking, but there's some evidence to indicate she might have been. For . . . as an example . . . say she had been drinking. She wouldn't want the police involved. Anyway, she tells Roger Lamott she has already called for a tow truck."

"Which she hasn't, and has no need of one," Merrick says.

"Right. There is no record that she called for any kind of assistance, and her car was drivable. In his statement Lamott says he could see how a big bearded trucker could be scary to a young woman on a dark highway so he agrees to leave, but as he pulls away slowly, he watches her in his mirrors, and quickly calls the police and lets them know what has happened."

"He says he was worried about her, and even though he said he wouldn't report the accident he did so anyway—for her safety."

"Now, from the time Lamott left Randa and called the police until the time they arrived was less than seven minutes," Daniel says.

"And it's important to note," Merrick adds, "that we don't just have Lamott's word for this, because the entire time from the accident when Randa got off the phone with her mom until a Gulf County sheriff's deputy arrived was only ten minutes."

"So we have two witnesses that help establish the timeline," Daniel says. "Three counting the deputy. To recap, from the time the dispatcher was called until the deputy arrived at Randa's car was less than seven minutes."

"Whatever happened to Randa Raffield happened in those seven minutes," Merrick says. "Because when the deputy arrived, she was gone and there was no trace of her. And there never has been again."

"Well," Daniel says, "there have been reported sightings over the years."

"True."

"The question is are any of them legit. We have no confirmed sightings of Randa. And we haven't even really started tracking down those who say they've seen her."

"Like the guy who swears she's a Vegas show-girl now," Merrick says. "Or the woman who said she saw Randa performing in a circus in Ohio. Or the Russian TV producer who says she's living in Russia and that he's got footage of her that he's soon going to reveal to the world."

"Yeah, like those. Of course, there are more credible reports than those, but none have been veri-fied or more importantly . . . produced Randa Raf-field."

"One final thing we should say in this recap is that the deputy found the business card of a tow-truck operator slipped into the driver's side window. The man, a . . . Donald Wynn . . . says in his statement to the police that he wasn't called by anyone, that he happened to be passing by, saw the car, stopped, didn't see anyone, then left his card in case the driver came back and needed help."

Turning on my flashers and turning off the car, I climb out and look around.

It's like so many rural North Florida roads—lined by pine trees and sand scrub undergrowth and not much else.

The area is empty, desolate—and would have been far more so back in 2005 at night.

I lift the phone to my ear to better hear the podcast as I walk around.

"Now, this part of Highway 98 was actually moved so that the St. Joe Company could have more land to develop," Merrick is saying.

"Really?" Daniel says. "I didn't know that."

"Yeah. When the St. Joe Company got out of the timber and paper industries, sold the mill and began to develop their coastal land, they asked and the obliging Gulf County Commissioners agreed to actually relocate the main highway to give them more private beach and bayfront property to develop. That's another issue in and of itself. The point I'm making right now is that there are pine woods on both sides of the road where Randa wrecked her car. Several places on 98 you can see the Gulf of Mexico on one side of the road, but here it's sand pine scrub on both sides."

"So it's like breaking down in the middle of the woods?" Daniel says.

"It's a lot like that, actually," Merrick says. "There are no houses, no buildings, no nothing. There is highway and there are pine woods. We're talking about one of the least developed parts of 98. The entire region is not very populated, but there's nobody along this part. We're talking between Mexico Beach and Port St. Joe. Behind the pines on one side is the Windmark Beach development, which was just really getting started back then, and beyond it the bay. And behind the pines on the other side is just more pines, more woods, and what locals call Panther Swamp. It goes on and on for miles and miles."

I look at what they're describing. If you don't know what's behind each one, and I doubt Randa did, you'd think you're deep in the middle of a dense pine forest.

Port St. Joe has long been a company town.

While South Florida was undergoing a land boom, the St. Joe Company, a company founded in 1936 as part of the Alfred I. du Pont trust and operated by his brother-in-law Edward Ball, purchased property in North Florida on the cheap. After the acquisition of a railroad and the construction of a paper mill, the newly formed company ushered in a new era in the Panhandle.

Smoke from the company's paper mill rose in the blue sky over St. Joseph Bay and the small town beneath it for most of a century, releasing sulfurous exhaust and other deadly toxins, and drawing some tens of millions of gallons of water a day from the Floridan aquifer, seriously depleting the water table.

Then, as the paper market began to soften, the St. Joe Company sold its mill and became a land developer, turning to planned communities like the one here at Windmark Beach.

Traffic is light, a few vehicles breezing by intermittently.

I cross the road to examine the guardrail on the other side. The spot where Randa hit it is still bent and bears a hint of the green paint of her car.

As I start to cross back over, the sheriff pulls up in her black SUV with her light bar on.

Chapter Three

"I see Merrick talked to you," she says, climbing down out of her vehicle and closing the door.

I nod. "Took me to lunch and made a compelling pitch."

Reggie Summers, the governor-appointed sheriff of Gulf County, is a muscular mid-forties woman with a widish frame, a darkish complexion, long, straight dirty-blond hair, and striking gray-green eyes. As usual, she's in jeans, boots, and a button-down shirt. No makeup or jewelry and her hair is pulled back in a ponytail.

"Thought you were in PC with your mom?" I say as we step over and lean against my car.

"Doctor got called into emergency surgery so they had to reschedule her appointment. I was headed back to the office when I saw your car."

We are quiet a moment as she looks around.

"So beautiful here," she says.

"Certainly is."

"So you found my Merrick compelling, huh?"

I smile. "It's an interesting case. I was just listening to their podcast when you pulled up."

She shakes her head, frowns, then slowly half smiles. "Used to think the only thing worse than a family member of a victim trying to investigate was a damned armchair detective, but . . . they're doing a really good job with it. It's convinced me they can be beneficial."

I nod. "Adnan Syed is getting a new trial thanks to *Serial* and *Undisclosed.*"

"It's a new day," she says. "Don't get me wrong, there's some bad shit and horrible misinformation out there. And there's plenty of cranks and crazies gettin' in the way of actual crime solving . . ."

"No doubt," I say. "There's far more bad than good online, far more that is useless and negative and worse than . . . anything else, but the handful of serious podcasts I've listened to are asking the right questions and maybe even finding new evidence and breathing new life back into cold cases."

She nods. "I agree. Some of it seems beneficial. Just not sure over all if it's going to do more harm than good."

"Will probably do plenty of both."

"Too true. What'd you tell Merrick about helping?"

"That I'd talk to you. Your department. Your call."

"I feel like he's putting you in a difficult position, and I told him. I want you to be honest with me and not do something you don't want to do or not do something you want to do because he's my . . . whatever he is. Will you be honest with me?"

"I will."

"Do you want to investigate it?"

"I do. But only officially. Only as an open un-solved case for the Gulf County Sheriff's Department. That's why it's your call."

"But you want to?"

"Yes."

"What are you working on right now?"

I had recently returned from vacation time I'd used to help my dad work an old case and didn't have a whole lot going.

"The Larcy fraud case and two other cold cases—the one involving your predecessor and the Remington James case you gave me. But I've barely started reading them. Haven't done any investigating so far."

"Why do you want to work the Raffield one?" she asks.

"It's gone unsolved too long. And I think Merrick and Daniel have uncovered details, facts, and maybe even evidence that wasn't known before."

"So you really want to work it?"

I nod. "I don't feel any pressure from you to say what I think you want me to."

"But if I say no, you won't do it?"

"Right."

"What if you really think you should and I still say no?"

I think about it. "I'd try to talk you into it. Failing that, I'd let it go or resign and work it on my own."

She nods and studies me for a long moment.

"What is it?" I ask.

"I'm around men who really have major problems with women in authority all the time. Many of them in my own department. But you don't."

I nod. "I don't."

"It's rare and refreshing. But it's curious."

"Curious?"

"Given what you've shared about your mom's addiction and your relationship with her."

"Ah. Yeah, I guess it is."

"Why? How'd you . . ."

I shrugged. "Probably not just one thing."

"Am I embarrassing you?"

I shrug. "A little."

"I'm really, really interested. I mean, it's one thing to respect women, but a corn-fed country bumpkin like me?"

I shake my head. "I hope your self-deprecation is just a shtick."

It's true that Reggie is a cowboy boot–wearing, Reba-loving, small-town country girl with a thick Southern drawl who occasionally uses improper grammar, but those things are endearing and charming, and could only obscure how strong and smart she is from those who lack perception or only have a fraction of her intelligence.

"So your ease and respect for women isn't the result of just one thing. Okay, so name a few for me. Please."

"Part of it is innate. How I arrived. Part of it's my concept of the divine."

"Yeah. I've heard you call God *she* and *mother*. Was going to ask you about that too one day."

"It's just the conception that the divine is no more male than female, but encompasses both masculinity and femininity. It's a very simple concept. First the natural then the spiritual. Nature is the pattern."

She nods and seems to think about it. "What else?"

"My relationship with my grandmothers, my sister Nancy, my friend Merrill's mom, and Anna. Anna's a huge part of it—and has been since childhood. And before she died—and even since—I've worked through some of the shit with my mom."

"Thank you. Thanks for sharing that with me. And thanks for the way you respect me. A lot of people respect you, they watch you, they see how you treat me. It helps."

"You're welcome."

"More men like you, and our next president would be female," she says.

We are in the height of a contentious and heated presidential election campaign between Hillary Clinton and Donald Trump.

"She's ahead in all the polls," I say.

"No way she wins," she says. "No way. And not just because of her failings as a candidate, the decades-long smear campaign she's been subjected to, or the fact that she's the establishment candidate in a change election year. It's that she's a woman. If there's one thing we are more than racist, it's sexist."

If she's right and the first female nominee of a major party running for president loses, it won't just be because she's a woman. There will be a million different factors, but she's right that ingrained and internalized sexism will be one of them—a big one.

"I'd say you were right if she were running against anyone else. He's . . . he's already disqualified himself in dozens of different ways."

"We'll see. Okay, so, yes. Let's reopen the Randa Raffield case and solve the thing this time. Can't have a couple of amateurs solving our cases— even if one of them is my . . . whatever he is."

Chapter Four

After leaving the place where Randa disappeared, I drive down 98, turn on Overstreet, and head to Wewa and Gulf Correctional Institution, listening to another episode of *In Search of Randa Raffield* as I do.

"On this episode we're going to talk about the various theories floating out there," Daniel says. "But before we do that we have a short segment with a very special guest on the phone."

"Yes, we do," Merrick says. "We're very excited to bring you Ashley Gaines. Ashley was a friend and classmate of Randa's at the University of West Florida, and has some important reminders we need to hear."

"She does," Daniel says, "and while we're on the subject of reminders, let me add that Merrick and I are not in law enforcement. Interestingly, we're both with women who are. My wife's an FDLE agent and his is a sheriff. But we're not detectives—private or otherwise."

"We've both done a fair amount of investigating," Merrick says. "Me as a journalist and Daniel as a profiler and consultant in crimes with ritualistic or religious elements. But we're not cops and we're not doing this show as anything but interested and concerned citizens."

"And we're doing it to share important information and uncover new evidence if we can," Daniel says. "To make sure no one forgets that Randa is still missing and her family and friends have no peace yet."

"With that in mind, let's welcome Ashley Gaines to the show," Merrick says. "Welcome Ashley. Thanks for being with us today."

"Thank you, Merrick, Daniel. I appreciate what you're doing and I thought this was the place to share what I have to share. Other shows have asked me to be on—other blogs and documentaries and news shows have tried to interview me, but I've said no to everyone but you guys."

"And why is that?" Merrick asks.

"Your sincerity, your respect for Randa. You're not treating this like light entertainment like so many are."

"And that's part of what you wanted to share, isn't it?" Daniel says.

"It is," she says. "Randa was a real person. A beautiful person. And not just outwardly with that shiny auburn hair, perfect porcelain skin, and those magnificent green eyes, but inwardly too. She had a truly beautiful soul. What happened to her—whatever it was—is real and tragic and heartbreaking and devastating to those of us who knew and loved her. Randa was a good person. Liked. Respected. She was a loving daughter. A good friend. Good student and athlete. She was one of the smartest people I've ever met and she had a very strong moral code. And some of the awful and bizarre things being said about her are just .

. . un . . . conscionable. She deserves better than that. Her death is not cheap entertainment. It's not a soap opera. It's—"

"So you believe Randa is dead?" Merrick says.

"There's no doubt in my mind," she says. "I think someone attacked her, took her, but she would have fought—she's strong, she's fierce. No way she'd be held captive. She would've fought him and . . . Anyway, that's all I wanted to say . . . that Randa was a good and loyal friend, a really good person, and she needs to be treated as such."

"Absolutely," Daniel says. "She—"

Ashley disconnects the call.

"Ashley?" Merrick says. "I guess she's gone. We had a few more questions, but . . . maybe we can do those at a later time."

"I think today she just wanted to make her statement," Daniel says. "Give everyone that important reminder. And it is important to remember that everyone we talk about on this show are real people. Randa is real. And while true crime and unsolved mysteries can have an element of entertainment in them, we're not doing this for entertainment. We're trying to find Randa. Find out what happened to her. Get her some justice and her family some peace. So . . . should we talk about the theories of what happened to her?"

"Theories of what happened to Randa," Merrick says. "And there are lots and lots of them."

"There are, but if you boil them all down to just the essentials," Daniel says, "you only have a few possibilities. I mean in terms of broad categories."

"Explain what you mean."

"There are tons of theories on how and why and who, but if we set those aside for a moment and just look at the broad categories, this is what we have: Randa could have run away. That's what she could have been doing anyway—so far from where she's supposed to be, on her own—and when she wrecked her car, she kept going, just on foot."

"Okay."

"Or hitched a ride with someone. Either way, she could have run away."

"So number one is she could have left on her own," Merrick says.

"Yes. Number two is she could have been taken. Someone came along and took her, forcibly, against her will. She didn't want to go, but . . . she was forced to."

"Okay, so are you saying those are the two main categories of what could have happened?"

"Actually, I think there are four—again, in the broadest sense. Homicide, suicide, accident, or she went into hiding," Daniel says. "We've seen things in her background, in the days and months leading up to her disappearance, that seem to point to the possibility of each one of those—and we'll get into her background later, in a future episode. But for now let's just say that all four are possibilities and I wanted to start as broad as we can and then narrow down from there."

"While we're staying broad," Merrick says, "take us through each of the four possibilities."

"Let's start with homicide," Daniel says. "Randa was murdered by someone—someone with her, someone following her, or someone who happened along."

"And we should say that we don't know if anyone was with her or following her or if anyone other than the two men we've already mentioned happened along—but there's evidence to suggest each one of these possibilities should at least be considered."

"Right."

Of course there's evidence to support all the theories. There always is. The problem with evidence is usually not how much or how little, but how it's interpreted. Evidence can be made to say nearly anything—unless it's allowed to speak for itself.

As I drive down Overstreet listening, my mind is on fire with the mystery of Randa Raffield. I want to hear more evidence, want to go over all the evidence, want to explore all the possibilities.

"We'll get into the odds of a murderer happening along within that narrow window of time," Daniel is saying.

"Seven minutes," Merrick says. "Or less. Could a killer have come along within those seven minutes and killed Randa?"

"And if he did, where is the body? Where is the evidence of a violent crime?"

"If she was murdered, it's far more likely that it was by someone with her or following her than someone who happened upon her, but we have to consider all three."

"And when we say following her," Daniel adds, "it doesn't have to be someone who followed her all the way from her dorm or from Pensacola. He could have seen her at one of her stops and started following her then."

"We know she stopped for gas and liquor not too far from where she wrecked and disappeared."

"Yes," Daniel says, "we have receipts and eye-witness statements and it's rumored the police have surveillance video footage, though we've never seen anything like that."

"Again," Merrick says, "we'll get into all of this later, but . . . maybe Randa wrecked because someone saw her at the gas station or liquor store and did something to her car and followed her, waiting for her to break down or wreck, and then attacked her."

"Okay," Merrick says, "that's homicide. How about suicide?"

"Let's say that was her plan all along," Daniel says. "She's hundreds of miles from where she's supposed to be because she was planning to do herself harm. And when she wrecked, she abandoned her car for some reason but didn't abandon her plan to kill herself."

"She could have walked through the woods and the Windmark Beach subdivision and into the bay and drowned herself. She could have walked into the woods on the other side and into Panther Swamp and slit her wrists or . . . harmed herself in some other way."

"But in either case," Daniel says, "we'd expect to find a body—in the bay or in the swamp—and no remains have ever been found."

"There was a massive search for Randa right when this happened," Merrick says, "and some of her friends and family are still searching, still showing up every so often to walk through the woods or boat across the bay to look for her."

"And nothing was ever found, has ever been found, in all that time."

"Were there things in Randa's background that would indicate she was suicidal?" Merrick asks.

"Possibly," Daniel says. "And we'll get into them later. Nothing overt or obvious, but maybe some things that hint at it."

"Okay. That's homicide and suicide. How about accident?"

"Same as some of the scenarios we've already mentioned," Daniel says, "but instead of someone intentionally killing her or her killing herself, it happens accidentally. Let's say the reason she left her car was that she was drinking and didn't want to get a DUI. People who are drinking and get into an accident often do this. They get away from the vehicle so when the cops come they're not there and can't get charged with a DUI. Later, they can come pick up the car at the impound lot and pay the fines or whatever and say that the car was stolen. Something like that. So say she left the car. And started walking. And steps out in front of a vehicle and is hit. She'd still be killed but by accident, but the driver doesn't want to deal with all that goes along with it, with even an accident, so buries her body. Or she walks into the woods and gets bitten by a cottonmouth moccasin. Or she decides to sober up by swimming in the bay and drowns."

"But in those last scenarios where is the body?" Merrick says.

"Exactly. Maybe just not found yet, but . . ."

"And that is possible. It's a huge, huge swamp. No way every inch of it has been searched—and even if it has, the body could have been missed and now the remains are such that they'd be even harder to find."

"Way harder. Not to mention animals could have scattered her remains."

"Exactly," Merrick says, "so we can't rule out any of those possibilities yet."

"Not yet, no."

"Okay, but let's say it wasn't murder or suicide or accident. What else could it have been?"

"Maybe she staged the whole thing and ran away. She could've had someone following her and they left together or she hitches a ride and never looks back. She could have taken a boat to Cuba or continued around the Gulf States and down into Mexico."

"It would explain why there's no body," Merrick says. "But again, we have to ask . . . were there things in Randa's background that would suggest she might do something like this, that she would even be capable? What do you think, Daniel?"

"Based on what we've seen, I'd say that every scenario we've discussed is at least a possibility, which is what makes this case so . . . interesting, compelling, maddening—take your pick."

"All of the above," Merrick says. "So, that's gonna do it for today. But keep tuning in because we're just getting started and we haven't even begun to delve deep into this riddle wrapped in a mystery inside an enigma."

"In future episodes of *In Search of Randa Raffield*," Daniel says, "we'll let you know all about her car—what was in it, what had been done to it, what happened to it, and where it is now. We'll examine Randa's background and any signs and clues that can shed light on what might have really happened to her. We'll interview people connected to the case—family, friends, cops, suspects."

"And," Merrick adds, "we'll take a closer look at her boyfriend and the rumor that she may have been stepping out on him even though they got engaged as the ball was dropping on New Year's Eve."

As the outro music begins to fade in, Daniel says, "All that and much more, coming up on *In Search of Randa Raffield*."

Chapter Five

Nearing Gulf Correctional Institution where I am a senior chaplain, I pull onto the shoulder of the empty rural road, put my car in Park, pop my trunk, place my weapon inside, and change into my clerical collar.

Firearms aren't permitted on state prison property. Other law enforcement officials arriving at the institution are required to check their weapons at the control room. Because I'm both employed here as a chaplain and at the Gulf County Sheriff's Department as an investigator, I obtained special permission from the warden and the secretary of the department of corrections to store my sheriff department–issued .40 caliber Glock and the small frame 9 mm I wear in an ankle holster in my trunk while on duty here.

Transition complete, I get back into my car and drive into the prison's employee parking lot.

I am in the odd and unique position, for me, of having two full-time jobs, and I'm not sure how much longer I can keep it up.

Over the course of my life, I've been officially a cop and unofficially a minister or officially a minister and unofficially an investigator, but now, for the first time, I am officially both. Though it seems to mostly be working, I constantly feel the tension between the two, the push and pull of each, and the squeeze of personal life and family time on both.

I find performing both jobs fulfilling, each rewarding in a way the other is not, each providing me with opportunities I feel called to, and doing both gives Anna the opportunity to stay home with Taylor—and Johanna when we have her—but I can't see being able to continue both for much longer.

I've talked to Anna about it—not only because of the toll it's exacting on me, but because I'm not sure I'm giving either job what it requires and deserves.

I enter the institution to the friendly greeting of "Chaplain" from my coworkers and the inmates in our care and custody, and think what a stark contrast from how I'm most often treated as a cop.

Of course, not every inmate is always happy to see me. I can't imagine the one I'm headed to see right now will show me anything but contempt and animosity.

I find Don Wynn behind the food services building, smoking the cheap, acrid tobacco sold in the canteen.

He's tall and thin with pale pasty skin and hair so closely cropped it's barely there.

Unlike many of the other neo-Nazis housed at GCI, the neck of Wynn's white skin holds no swastikas, eagles, lighting bolts, or Hitler heads, and there are no black or green teardrops at the corners of his bright blue eyes. He's too subtle for that, but he's one of the most committed, most true-believing, most vile racists and fascists on the compound.

He's alone among the empty cardboard boxes, food crates, trashcan casters, brooms, and mops, and nods at me when I walk up. "Chaplain."

I nod to him.

"What brings you back behind the slop shed?" he says.

"Looking for you."

"Found me."

His tone is light and insincere, indifferent, dismissive, and he doesn't really look at me so much as in my direction.

"Mind if I ask you a few questions?"

He becomes wary. "About?"

"The Randa Raffield case."

He nods and seems to think about it, scratching the stubble on his chin with a too-long thumbnail.

"Tell you what . . ." he says. "I'll answer your questions if you answer a few of mine."

"Okay."

"Why do you want to know?"

I had read his arrest report and inmate file. He had been convicted of aggravated assault, rape, and attempted murder of a young woman about Randa's age from the Springfield area in Panama City. As I read the report, I wondered how many other victims there had been, how many where murder wasn't just attempted, and if Randa had been one of them.

"We're reopening the case," I say.

"*We?*" he asks, his eyebrows shooting up, his deep blue eyes finding mine for the first time.

"Gulf County Sheriff's Department."

"You their chaplain too?"

"Investigator."

"Investigator? What? You a law dog *and* a convict chaplain?"

I nod.

"Well, damn. I mean . . . damn. That's . . . downright . . . unprecedented."

"It just may be, but I doubt it. So . . . you left your business card on Randa Raffield's car. Why?"

"Wasn't done asking my questions," he says. "But we can seesaw back and forth if you want. I owned my own tow truck. Well, the . . . ah . . . hook-nosed crooks at the bank owned it, but I . . . that's what I did at the . . . I had my own wrecker service. Needed business. Never been shiftless or lazy or corrupt. Never lived off the government."

"Until now," I say.

His eyes widen and a creepy smile spreads across his face. "This sure as shit ain't by choice. Anyway, I seen a car broke down on the side of the road and, as was my custom when it looked like the kind of car I towed, I stopped to see if I could be of assistance."

"The kind of car you towed?"

"Not too fancy, foreign, or uppity," he says. "None of that rigged or pimped-out shit."

Translation—no Jewish or African American–owned vehicles.

"Where were you headed? Where were you coming from?"

"Had just left Highland View where I lived at the time with my old lady and was headed to Millville for a meeting."

"What kind of meeting?"

"Kind true patriots attend. I was concerned with making America great way back then. I stopped. No one was around. I beeped my horn. Waited a few minutes. No one came out of the woods. Left my card on the car and left."

"You were driving your tow truck to your meeting?"

"Was the only vehicle I had."

"And you never saw anyone—the entire time you were there?"

He shakes his head.

"Which was how long?" I ask.

"Couple of minutes, max."

If he's telling the truth, it means Randa disappeared in even less than seven minutes. Less than five depending on how much time elapsed between him leaving and the deputy arriving. Of course, he could be lying. Or Roger Lamott could. Or they both could.

"Now I got a question for you," he says.

"Okay."

"How can you claim to be a man of God and let all those false religions defile the chapel the way you do?"

"I don't claim to be anything. And if you think your religion is the only true and right one, the only one worthy to use the chapel provided by the state of Florida for all those incarcerated here, then it's your religion you need to look at, not others."

He nods and looks as if I've just confirmed something for him.

"A change is comin'," he says. "It's already begun. Just you wait. You and all the other false prophets like you and all the mongrels will be cast out of the White House and God's house. You'll see."

"Did you kill Randa Raffield?" I ask. "Was she not pure enough for you? Did you rape her before or after you killed her?"

He shakes his head, nonplused. "Never raised my hand to any bitch. Never dicked one wasn't gaggin' for it neither."

"Your jacket says otherwise."

I study him but he gives nothing away.

"Think we're done here," he says, "but answer me one more question first. If I did it—and you ain't the first to say I did—why would I leave my business card on her car?"

"Before we started talking I would've said it was because you were smart enough to throw suspicion off yourself—to be able to say what you just did—but after hearing you speak I can clearly see that's not the case."

Chapter Six

Zaire Bell, a forty-something African-American beauty with caramel-colored skin, sparkling, wickedly intelligent black eyes, large, luscious brown lips, and a wavy afro extending six inches from her head, is a new doctor at the Sacred Heart Hospital in Port St. Joe and Merrill Monroe's new girlfriend.

Zaire, who goes mostly by Za, and Merrill and Anna and I are shooting darts at Tukedawayz Tavern, still full from the Tiki Grill food next door.

It's couple versus couple in an epic game of Cricket.

Merrill is drinking Bud Light from a bottle, the two women have wine, and I have Diet Coke over ice.

Eva Cassidy's haunting acoustic cover of "Ain't No Sunshine" is on the jukebox. Anna had played it for me when she and Za had fed a couple of paychecks into the machine when we first arrived.

It's a weeknight and the place is empty except for an older man nursing a Natty at the opposite end of the bar. He's a friend of the bartender, who is engaged in conversation with him, so it's like we have the place to ourselves.

We're here on a weeknight because of the alignment of Za's night off and our babysitter's availability—and because we get the place mostly to ourselves.

"I ran into Reggie at the IGA," Anna says. "She told me about your conversation."

Za stops shooting and turns around toward us. "Reggie, the sheriff?" she says. "I like her."

"She's John's boss," Anna says.

"I thought you worked at the prison," Za says to me.

"I do."

"But he's also an investigator with the sheriff's department," Anna says.

"Damn."

"Not doing a particularly great job at either of them right now," I say. "Will probably have to give up one before long."

"But which one?" Merrill says.

"Reggie was saying how tough it is to be a woman in that position," Anna says.

"Tell her try bein' a doctor—and a woman of color," Za says.

"She was saying how refreshing it was to have her lead investigator treat her with respect and dignity and without sexism or condescension."

Za nods and turns back and shoots her last dart.

Anna looks at me. "She said you gave me part of the credit for it."

I nod.

"Merrill's mom too," she says, looking from me to Merrill.

Merrill smiles—something he's doing far more of these days, something that coincided with the introduction of Zaire into his life.

Instead of gathering her darts and pressing the button for the next player, Za turns and says, "That's something I've been meaning to ask."

"The way into Mama Monroe's heart?" I say.

"No. How are you all the way you are? Serious question. I've never seen a place with such racism, sexism, and bigotry. And then there's you all."

"That's 'cause this your first visit to the Deep South," Merrill says.

"I'm from Miami," she says. "Harder to get more south than that."

"Deep South," Merrill says. "Confederate-forget-like-Hell-South's-gonna-rise-again Deep South. Not South Beach."

"Question stands. How can y'all be the way you are?"

"I owe it to Anna and Merrill," I say.

"I owe it to John," Anna says.

"Me too," Merrill says.

"Y'all are being flippant about something I'm really tryin' to understand."

"Sorry," I say.

"Me too," Anna says.

"I ain't," Merrill says, and takes a long pull on his bottle of Bud.

"You deserve a real answer," I say. "And I think Merrill should be the one to give it to you. But before he does, I should say that there's bigotry everywhere. I doubt there's more here than anywhere else. And like everywhere else there are some truly great people here. Probably more than most places."

"All true," Anna says. "And I agree. Merrill should have to answer. He's your date, after all."

Za looks at Merrill.

He sets his bottle on the small, round, high table and clears his throat.

"I'll do that thing you really like tonight if you give me a serious answer," she says to him.

"Forget the question," I say. "Let's talk about that."

"Yeah," Anna says, "what thing does he really like?"

"The question is," Merrill begins, serious now, "how does one grow up in a culture without adopting the biases, suppositions, conventions, assumptions, and general bigotry of that culture? And, of course, there's not just one answer. In my case, I'm part of the minority, so that gives me a certain sensitivity to the plight of the marginalized."

"And yet many minorities have bigoted attitudes toward other minority or marginalized groups," I say. "And I'd say you were born with the sensitivity."

He nods. "Some of us are more aware than others. See things. Read things. And you meet certain likeminded others who help. My relationship with John did that. In fact, as John was just saying, even as a member of the marginalized minority, I lacked compassion for another marginalized minority, namely the gays, and John helped me with that."

"Having a gay friend will do that," Anna says.

I smile.

"But it's so true," Za says. "I'm continually amazed at how many people who are the victims of bigotry are bigots to other groups themselves."

"Humans are tribal," Anna says. "Even those— sometimes especially those whose tribe has been shunned, abused, unfairly targeted."

"So true," Za says. "How about you?"

"I'm a woman," Anna says. "I've got a gay brother. John has been a big influence. I don't know . . ."

Za nods. "I can see why Merrill and Anna are the way they are. I mean, not all the reasons, but hints at some of the reasons, but you—" she says, looking at me "—how did you—"

"I'll take that one too," Merrill says, "but if I do, I better get that thing I like at least two times."

Za smiles.

"John is an enigma. A lot of the things you're asking about are just innate, just part of his moral DNA. And because of those he gravitated toward teachers who taught a message of equality and com- passion, the common-cup and open-table fellowship where everyone is welcomed. Teachers like Jesus and the Buddha, Rumi and MLK."

"Merrill could've been a professor if he wanted to," Anna says.

"Got one more thing to say," he says, "and then I'd really like to be done with this topic for to- night."

Za nods.

"Imagine having a heightened sensitivity to others, particularly the marginalized and the outcasts, the modern equivalent of lepers. If you have that kind of compassion and desire for justice for them, especially in a rural area where you won't encounter many others like yourself, don't you think that would make you feel like an outsider yourself? Don't you think someone like that wouldn't feel like they fit in here or much of anywhere—and wouldn't that add to and intensify the identification with and the compassion for those marginalized others?"

Anna takes my hand.

We are all quiet a moment, Za seeming to consider what Merrill has said.

"Now, shoot your damn darts so we can go back to your place and make good on your promise."

"Fuck darts," she says. "I've never been so turned on in my entire life. Let's go home now, you thug poet professor, you."

"Bye," Merrill says to us, a big smile spreading across his face.

As we embrace and they prepare to leave, Za says, "You all are very lucky to have each other."

"Yes, we are," I say.

They've only taken a few steps when Zaire turns back and says, "You all aren't leaving too?"

"Not quite yet," I say.

"We have to see a man about a horse," Anna says. "Well, a car."

When they are gone, Anna calls the bartender down to this end of the bar and distracts her while I move in to talk to Ty—just like we planned.

Ty McCann was the first deputy to arrive at the scene of Randa's abandoned car.

I ask him about it.

"It's so easy to look back on something in hindsight and criticize it," he says.

I nod.

His old face is pocked and pitted, and as he's aged, his nose and ears have grown, giving an exaggerated look to his face and its features.

"All these damn armchair detectives and their goddamn theories. Some of 'em suspect me. Actually accuse me of taking her and killing her."

"Really?"

"Yeah, say I got there before the tow-truck guy who left his card. Claim I had already taken her."

I shake my head.

"It's not an easy job, but . . . I was good at it, gave it my best every night. Did I make mistakes? Of course. But not many. And no big ones. No moral or ethical ones. And to be the subject of baseless theory bullshit . . . I was just a few days from retirement when all this happened. It's the last thing I ever worked. How I went out."

"Sorry."

"Yeah, well . . ."

"Would you mind taking me through that night?"

He takes another sip of his beer. "Nah, I don't mind."

The jukebox is still moving through the music Anna and Zaire selected earlier—REM's "Losing My Religion" is on now—and at the other end of the bar, Anna is listening to the bartender intently.

"I was at the sheriff's station when the call came in. From the time the call came to the time I pulled up in front of her car was less than seven minutes. No one was there. Not in the car. Not outside the car. Not on the street. Not in the woods right around the area. I looked everywhere."

I nod.

He's looking off into the distance now and I can tell he's back at the scene from that night.

"What about Windmark?" I ask. "Did you check in there?"

He shakes his head. "It was a little ways down 98 and all dark back in there. Wasn't much there at the time and . . . but I should have. I searched all around it, but . . . in hindsight should have gone all through it. That's on me. Just didn't know what I was dealing with."

The bartender grabs her cigarettes and lighter and heads out the back door. Anna joins us.

I introduce them and he continues.

"There was really no sign of an accident, not that I could see at first. Car looked fine. No signs of foul play. Just looked like a parked car. When something first happens, you can't tell what it'll become. Just no way to predict what it'll turn into." Anna nods and gives him an understanding look. "At the time I figured the driver had been drinking and didn't want to get a DUI. Figured she was hiding in the woods. Drunk drivers do that a lot. Leave their car. Come back to it later."

"That does happen a lot," I say.

"How was I supposed to know this was gonna turn into some big missing persons case that goes on forever? Don't know what I would've done different if I *had* known. I treated it like what it looked like. I treated it like what it would've been ninety-nine times out of a hundred. Anyway . . ."

"Did you see or hear anything, reach any conclusions—then or later—that are not in your report?"

He shakes his head. "It's all in there. 'Cause there wasn't much to it. The scene I mean. And I'm not gonna offer any more stupid useless fuckin' theories, but I'll tell you this—everybody says she was abducted, right? That some killer came along and took her. But if that's the case, why was her car locked?"

"You're sure her car was locked?" I ask.

"Positive. That's why I thought she was just hiding somewhere."

Chapter Seven

"I'm so happy for Merrill," Anna says. "I really like Zaire."

"You're okay with him not ending up with Zadie Smith?"

She laughs. "I had forgotten that. Yeah, Zadie would've been nice, but Zaire is great."

We are driving home from Tucks in her Mustang beneath a huge harvest moon. I'm driving and she's leaning on the center console toward me. Her breath smells of fruit. It's the aroma it gets when she drinks wine, the aroma I associate with amorousness and affection.

"I really enjoyed helping you tonight," she says. "Reminded me of the old days."

"It did," I say, nodding. "I've missed that. Didn't even realize how much."

"Maybe I could help you some more with this one," she says.

"Sure. I would love that."

"I love our lives—our *life*, guess it's one shared life now—and I'm so grateful for the time I get with Taylor, but . . . I'm gettin' a little . . . restless . . . and it'd help to have something to do other than diapers and dishes."

"It would help me," I say.

"I started listening to the podcast already," she says. "It's sort of addicting. Anyway, I think I'm caught up to where you are. I wouldn't mind if you wanted to turn it on now."

I smile and turn on the podcast.

"So," Merrick is saying, "the initial investigation was fraught with . . . well . . . fuckups. The first deputy on the scene . . . didn't do much."

"We should say his name is Ty McCann," Daniel says. "He thought someone had just left their car on the side of the road. Either that it was broken down or the driver was drunk and left the scene to avoid getting a DUI."

"These were reasonable assumptions," Merrick says.

"Yeah, it's easy to look back now and point out all he did wrong, but . . ."

"I want to address something right here before we go on," Merrick says. "There are theories floating out there that say Deputy McCann took Randa, but there's not a single piece of evidence that suggests anything like that. And this is the point I want to make—a theory with not a single shred of evidence, with nothing behind it to even suggest it could at least be a possibility, is useless, juvenile, and silly."

"It's like saying Bigfoot took her or that she spontaneously combusted—both of which are actual theories with apologists online. The point is you can *say* anything but we're not going to give any credence to the outlandish and fanciful if they have no evidence undergirding them."

"Now," Merrick adds, "we're going to look at every possibility—even the farfetched—but if there's nothing to suggest that they could possibly be true, we won't be covering them on our show. We're not going to waste your or our time. If there's evidence that Deputy McCann had anything to do with Randa's disappearance then we'll look at it, but we're not going to accuse him or speculate about him just because he was the first officer on the scene."

"So back to the initial investigation," Daniel says. "Deputy McCann thought it was just a parked car. He did a search around the area. Saw no sign of the driver or anyone else. No sign of foul play."

"So he has the car towed . . . and that's really about it. Until two days later when her family reports her missing and everybody begins to question why she was three-hundred miles from where she was supposed to be."

"What we're saying is the investigation started two days late," Daniel says. "Once it started, it seems like it was thorough and sound, but . . . losing two entire days . . ."

"Hard to overcome that kind of deficit," Merrick says. "The cops went back to the area. Turned it into a crime scene. There was a massive search for Randa—in the woods, along the highway, in Panther Swamp, in the bay, on Cape San Blas. Dogs were brought in. At first search dogs. Then later cadaver dogs. And not only was there a massive search then, Randa's family—and we'll be getting into Randa's fascinating family in a later show—has continued to search for her."

"And there's never been a single piece of evidence," Daniel says. "Not a trace, not a sign—nothing, not then and not since—that shows she was ever there."

"She literally vanished off the face of the earth," Merrick says. "If she wound up in the bay, her body would've washed up at some point. If she died in the swamp, there's a good chance the searchers would have found her. So . . . given that, you might say, well, someone took her, but how in less than seven minutes and maybe as few as five did a killer happen to be passing by just at the right moment? Can you imagine the odds, the timing, of that happening? It's astronomical. And don't forget she had just refused help from Roger Lamott. Can't see her getting in the car with someone else. At least not willingly."

"But," Daniel says, "there is some evidence that may indicate that's exactly what happened. Well, not the willingly part."

"You're talking about the search dogs, right?" Merrick says.

"Uh huh. Search dogs picked up her scent near where her car was and followed it down the side of the highway about fifty yards or so and then . . ."

"Lost the scent."

"Right. It didn't go into the woods on either side. Didn't double back or keep going. It just stopped."

"Like she got into a car."

"Like she got into a car," Daniel repeats.

"And maybe she did," Merrick says, "but . . . after two days . . . with a good hard rain and all those people stomping around the crime scene . . . it's possible the dog just lost the scent—or that it was gone."

I stop the podcast and turn off the car.

Anna shakes her head and says, "What do you think happened to her?"

I shrug. "Don't have nearly enough yet to even hazard a guess."

"Well, you're the only one. You should read the shit online."

"No I shouldn't and neither should you."

She smiles. "Can't help myself. Speaking of . . . Can we listen to some more while we fall asleep?"

Chapter Eight

After paying the babysitter, I called Johanna while Anna put Taylor to bed. Now, after making love, we are in our bed about to listen to more of the podcast.

"Be honest," I say. "Did it cross your mind to ask if we could listen to it while we were making love?"

She smiles her plead-the-fifth smile and changes the subject. "How was Johanna?"

"Good. Sleepy. Excited to be coming this weekend."

"Can't wait 'til she's here. Wish we had her all the time."

"I know you do, and I appreciate that more than you know. Thank you for how good you are with her."

"She's our girl. Just like Taylor. Thank *you* for how good you are with her."

"I love our family."

"I do too," she says. "Can you imagine being Randa Raffield's parents?"

I shake my head and actually shudder a little bit, shaking the bed. "I feel so . . . I don't have a word for what I feel for them."

"Wonder if they appreciate all the attention Randa and her case are getting or if they feel exploited?"

"They've not said anything publicly, but I plan to ask them when I talk to them."

"That's right," she says. "You're official. Unlike all the amateur sleuths working this thing, you can talk to them. Guess I'm not quite used to you being official yet. Wonder how Merrick and Daniel will really feel if you solve it? I know they say they just want it solved, but I wonder if they really want to be the ones who solve it."

"Bet it's both. I'm sure they'll be very happy for the case to be cleared no matter who does it—especially Merrick if it's Reggie's department that does it—but I'm sure they'd love to be the ones to solve it. Any sleuth, armchair or otherwise, would want to."

"Who do you think wants to be the one who solves it more, them or you?"

"It's not even close. Me."

"Well, let's listen so you can," she says.

I turn on the podcast.

"Before we start today's show, we need to say a few things," Merrick says.

"Yes we do," Daniel says. "We are united on this and we have a very strong resolve."

"We're not going anywhere," Merrick says. "We won't be intimidated or threatened or bullied off this case."

"No we won't," Daniel adds.

"And we're not talking to our critics or even the trolls out there in the anonymity of the internet."

"We can handle criticism. We can handle you disagreeing with us—what we're doing, how we're doing it. Even when you do it disagreeably."

"Right. We're not talking to our critics and detractors. We're talking to those actually threatening us, those of you who wish harm upon us and our families."

"We've received threatening phone calls, emails, letters, messages, and now even videos that show our loved ones—as if they're being stalked, telling us to back off or we'll know what it's like to lose a loved one too."

I stop the podcast and call Merrick.

"You okay?" I say.

"Yeah, why?"

"I was just listening to the podcast and heard about the threats."

"Oh, yeah. We're fine. That was a while back. Reggie looked into it. Think you were away helping your dad with the Bundy case or something."

"What'd she find out?"

"Nothing. We're being extra careful. Think it's just an internet troll who took it too far. Looks like the pictures and footage in the video is all from Facebook and other online places, but the way he edited it, it looks like he shot it and was stalking us. It's crazy how many crazies there are around this case, man. And I have no doubt some of them are truly dangerous—hell, it could even be Randa's killer for all we know. It's Daniel I feel bad for. Just him and Sam in that big, secluded house in Tallahassee."

"We'll figure something out for them," I say. "And we'll try to get to the bottom of who's behind it. Be extra careful until then."

"Dan and I both got concealed carry permits."

"Then be even extra, extra careful," I say.

He laughs. "We will. Reggie says her money's on one of us shooting ourselves before this is all over."

When we disconnect, I tell Anna what he said.

"Who would have the motive to do something like that besides the killer?"

"Could truly just be a crazy. We need to find out. Want to listen to more or did you get sleepy?"

"Please, sir, I want some more," she says in her best British accent, which isn't very good.

"It's interesting how bad that was and how turned-on I am," I say, and start the podcast again.

"So what do we actually know about Randa Raffield's family?" Merrick says.

"Before we get into that," Daniel says, "we should clear something up that seems to be causing a lot of confusion. There's a Raffield Fisheries located in Port St. Joe just a few miles from where Randa went missing. And some people believe she was headed there—or to see some of the Raffields in the area. They're a big family in Port St. Joe. But Randa Raffield isn't related to any of the Raffields that live in Port St. Joe."

"Again, one of the biggest theories floating around online is that she was related to them and on her way to see them," Merrick says, "but it's just incorrect. She is no relation to the Raffields of Port St. Joe."

"Now that we've cleared that up, let's talk about her family," Daniel says. "Randa's mom and dad, Lynn and Jerry Raffield, divorced when she was fifteen—something that by all accounts was very difficult for her."

"Yes," Merrick says. "Until that happened she was a straight-A student, a star swimmer for her high school, a very happy, carefree young woman."

"And it wasn't like she completely changed after her parents split up."

"Not at all. She just lost her way a little. Wasn't as happy. Didn't make as good of grades. Got into a little trouble here and there. Again, nothing major, but enough to contrast how she had been before."

"Randa grew up in Fort Walton Beach," Daniel says. "After the divorce, she and her mom, who by the way didn't change her name and didn't plan to until Randa was grown, stayed in Fort Walton, while Jerry, her dad, moved out to Seaside."

"Seaside of *The Truman Show* fame," Merrick says.

"Yes, the planned community along 30A where Jim Carrey's movie *The Truman Show* was shot. A place Merrick and I couldn't afford to live."

"No doubt," Merrick says. "Now think about this, on the night she disappeared, Randa, who was supposed to be in Atlanta, had to pass by both her mom's place and her dad's place on her way to wherever she was heading."

"That's right," Daniel says. "I never thought of it quite that way. But you're—but how do we know she didn't stop?"

"Just going by the official statements. Neither parent saw her that night—according to them. And we know her mom was on the phone with her at the time of the accident, but she thought it was in Atlanta or on the way back."

"So . . . Randa's mom is a minister at a small New Thought church called Unity of Fort Walton," Daniel says. "She's been there a long time—most of Randa's childhood and adolescence. She took a short break after Randa disappeared but is still the minister there."

"New Thought? What is that?"

"A relatively recent philosophical and spiritual movement that says stuff like Infinite Intelligence is supreme, universal, and everlasting, that divinity dwells in everyone, that the highest spiritual principle is love, and that most of our problems and issues are a result of the shit we think."

"Gotcha. Okay. Now . . . Jerry Raffield is a licensed clinical psychologist in private practice and he writes pop psychology books of the self-help variety. We should note that his mom left him the house in Seaside and some money when she passed away, which is how he's able to afford to live there."

"From what we can gather," Daniel says, "it looks like Lynn wanted the divorce and Jerry didn't, but still, he felt bad for how it affected Randa and tried to make it up to her in a variety of ways."

"He indulged and pampered her," Merrick adds.

"Looks like it, yes. And we'll get into that more when we look at Randa's background and its possible impact on what happened to her."

"We'll try to suss out any clues that might help us solve the case," Merrick says. "Not only in her background, but specifically in the weeks and days leading up to her disappearance."

"Yes, she had a lot going on," Daniel adds. "Which may be suggestive."

Anna taps my arm and I stop the podcast. "You falling asleep?" I ask.

"No, not yet. Just wanted to say, don't you think Merrick and Daniel are doing a great job? It's so smooth and conversational, so easy to listen to."

"Really is," I say. "Merrick was saying to me given the state of journalism and the crisis in print media, he thought that this part of his life was over and he didn't know what he was going to do. I think this is a perfect fit for him."

"And it's got to be good for poor Daniel," she says.

"Speaking of . . . Given the threats they're receiving and how much is on him in taking care of Sam, I'm gonna see if he'd move over here, closer to us, closer to Merrick and Reggie, Merrill and Zaire, even Dad and Verna—figure we could all keep an eye on them and help him with her."

"That's a great idea. Think he will?"

"If we find the right situation for them. I'm looking."

"Let me know what I can do," she says.

Though my first inclination is to say she has enough on her with taking care of a baby and sometimes a young child, I recall what she said earlier about feeling restless and instead say, "I will. I'll need your help."

"Just name it."

"I will. Thanks. Want to listen to some more or are you—"

"Think I'm too sleepy now," she says, trying to stifle a yawn. "You go ahead. I know you need to get through it as quickly as you can. I'll catch up tomorrow while Taylor naps."

I lean over and kiss her goodnight, then retrieve my headphones from the table, and in the darkness of our bedroom with my future wife sleeping next to me, dive back into the rabbit hole that is the Randa Raffield case.

Chapter Nine

"Jerry and Lynn Raffield have not only contradicted each other, they've contradicted themselves," Merrick says.

"They've both made similar statements, believed similar things—but never at the same time—and they've both changed what they initially said they thought it was."

"Jerry's first statements indicated he thought Randa intended herself harm, that whatever she was doing on that barren stretch of 98, wherever she was headed, it was to end her life."

"And there were items in her car that suggest he might be right," Daniel adds. "We'll get into that in our 'Randa's Car' episode, but I just wanted to mention that there is some other evidence—both in Randa's behavior and things in her car—that indicate Jerry might be right."

"Yes, and we'll get to those very soon," Merrick says. "As for Lynn, she first said that Randa had confided in her that she thought she might be being stalked and she, Lynn, was convinced that someone took her daughter. Said Randa had no intentions of doing herself harm. And here again . . . there is indeed evidence that indicates maybe Randa was being stalked. She was definitely having guy problems."

"So," Daniel says, "the question is, who knew more about their daughter at the time of her disappearance?"

"You would think a distinguished psychologist would know if someone was suicidal," Merrick says, "but your own family members are often the most difficult to diagnose."

"And in general," Daniel says, "I'd expect a daughter that age to be closer to her mother. Maybe she had confided things to her that she hadn't yet shared with her dad."

"But there is some question about whether she was close to either one of them at the time she vanished."

"Some of her friends said she had withdrawn from everyone but her boyfriend—including her parents—which . . . I mean . . . she passed by both of their places that night without stopping to see either one, so . . ."

"As far as we know," Merrick adds.

"Yes, as far as we know. But then both her parents seemed to change their story."

"Yes," Merrick says. "So, at first Jerry indicated Randa intended to harm herself, but then the very next day, he made statements to the media that his daughter was missing, someone had her, and he criticized the Gulf County Sheriff's Department for not doing more to find her and get her back."

"Some have theorized that Jerry changed his story because someone had convinced him that law enforcement would do more to find an abducted girl than one who went off to do herself in."

"And that's probably right," Merrick says. "But that's just a guess on our part. We don't really know. Maybe Jerry learned something else about this daughter that made him change his mind. Maybe Lynn convinced him. Maybe he . . . who knows."

"Then later," Daniel says, "both parents seemed to suggest that they thought both scenarios were possible. Lynn made statements that seem to indicate she was at least open to the idea that her daughter wanted to harm herself—though she said if she did it was because of her stalker and not because of the other reasons and theories people believe about Randa and her compromised mental state."

"Eventually, Jerry too indicated that it could be either—though it really did seem that whatever one parent said, the other would contradict, that they would go back and forth like that."

"But," Daniel adds, "eventually they both stopped communicating with the press or police. They each were on one of those true crime TV shows at about the five- and ten-year marks, though different shows, but nothing since and nothing in between. And they both have attorneys that do all their speaking for them."

"Which," Merrick says, "has caused some to suspect them—and not just because of that, but different things about them and the way they've acted. But those are just theories and rumors. No law enforcement agency has ever indicated Jerry and Lynn were suspects."

"But here's perhaps the strangest thing about them and why so many people familiar with the case say something is off about Jerry and Lynn," Daniel says. "They had a very large life insurance policy on their daughter, who, we should remind everyone, was their only child."

"And when could they collect on that policy?" Merrick asks.

"That's where it gets very interesting," Daniel says. "In most states, a missing person can be declared dead—I think the legal term is something like *death in absentia*—after seven years, though in some states it's shorter. As short as four years, but for most it's seven. It's even shorter if the missing person was in a situation that involved what they call *imminent peril*—like a plane crash, a bad storm, or terrorist attack. But in the vast majority of cases, it's seven years."

"Are there a lot of these type cases?" Merrick asks.

"I believe estimates are that there have been somewhere between fifty thousand and one hundred thousand in the US."

"And what has to happen for a missing person to be declared dead?" Merrick asks.

"An interested party, such as the parents in this case, has to petition the court to declare the missing person dead by assumption. There are several criteria that have to be met—such as the person's absence has to be continuous and inexplicable. Like they didn't just run away from money problems, impending indictment, or a bad relationship. There can have been no communication from the person. And a search for the person has to have taken place—a diligent search and investigation into the person's whereabouts."

"And were all of those criteria met?"

"Yes. Almost five years ago now."

"And did Jerry and Lynn have their daughter declared dead?"

"No, they did not," Daniel says. "Which begs the question, why have this huge life insurance policy on a child and then not collect on it when you're legally entitled to?"

"Yeah, that is . . . Jerry and Lynn are interesting people. Wish we could talk to them. Wish they were still talking to anyone. But that's not the end of the story, is it?"

"No, it's not," Daniel says. "Randa's parents didn't petition the court to have her declared dead, but someone else did. And we'll talk about who on our next show."

Chapter Ten

When I open my eyes the next morning, Anna is looking down at me, her big brown eyes bright and sparkling with desire.

"Feel like making love before you get ready for work?" she asks.

"Is that a trick question?"

"I woke you up a little early so we could."

"How much early?" I ask.

"Just fifteen minutes."

"Then we don't have any time to waste."

We didn't waste any time in starting our day in the very best way possible.

Afterward, she walks in as I shower.

"How far'd you get last night?" she asks.

"On the podcast? Just another episode."

"So you ended not knowing who petitioned the court to declare Randa dead? How could you go to sleep not knowing?"

"Actually think I fell asleep before the end of that episode. Not sure, but think the outro music and credits coming on woke me up."

"Can I tell you? Can I tell you?"

"Who petitioned the court? Of course."

She pulls back the shower curtain and sticks her head in.

"How long have you been up?" I ask.

"Which time? This last time since about five."

"Sorry."

"I love it. It's my job. Plus, the chance to help you with this has me energized like a mofo."

"So who petitioned the court?" I say.

"Scarlett George."

"What is a Scarlett George?"

"A suspect, in my book," she says.

"Who is she? Is it a she?"

"*She* is Lynn Raffield's sister, Randa's aunt. She's estranged from the family—bet you anything there's a story there. She wasn't allowed around Randa. There's all kinds of speculation about her online, but I'm just beginning to look through it."

"Would you mind seeing what else is out there?" I ask. "Online, I mean. Blogs. Podcasts. Reddit groups."

"Already on it. We'll have a lot to talk about at dinner."

"Thank you."

"And I think I found a place for Daniel and Sam to stay."

"Randa drove a 2004 deep green pearl Honda Accord EX sedan," Merrick is saying. "She got it in the fall of 2004 as a gift from Jerry Raffield, her dad, so it was just a few months old the night she vanished."

I'm driving south on 71 toward work, listening to another episode of Merrick and Daniel's podcast, a sausage biscuit and Diet Coke my only companions.

"Today on the show we're going to talk about Randa's car and what was in it," Daniel says.

"Daniel, has anyone, including your parents, ever just given you a brand new car?"

"No, Merrick, I've never had that particular experience. How about you?"

Merrick laughs. "No, me neither. So . . . not only is it an enormous gift and shows how indulgent Jerry could be, but from what we've gathered, Randa really didn't need a new car when he got it for her."

"She was driving a relatively new 2002 aspen green pearl Toyota Camry at the time, which he had also gotten her new, and there was nothing wrong with it."

"What is it with this girl and green cars?" Merrick says.

"They're not just both green. They're practically the same car."

"That's true. They're very, very similar cars. Easy to mistake for each other. So a few more points about the car. It was new. There was nothing wrong with it. It was drivable after the accident. So there was no need to call the police or a wrecker service."

"So why did she?" Daniel says.

"She didn't," Merrick says.

"No, I know she didn't make the calls. I'm saying why did she tell Roger Lamott she called a tow— but beyond that, why get out of a drivable car and stand on a dark highway at night when you could've kept driving?"

"Why not get back into it the moment Lamott pulls off and drives away?" Merrick says. "Doesn't make sense."

"Unless," Daniel says, "she was just so upset, so shaken up from the accident that she didn't realize she could just drive away."

"Or she was dazed and out of it because she smacked her head on the steering wheel or window or something and was just confused."

"Right. We just don't know. We don't know why she would get out of her car. We don't know why she would stay out. Like so many things about this case, it makes no sense."

"So we don't know why she got out or stayed out," Merrick says. "But let's talk about what we do know. We know that Randa was indulged by her dad."

"Or . . . to frame it a different way," Daniel says, "a father who has plenty of money trades in her current car for a new car every two years—to keep her safe and in something dependable. And who knows—maybe it's good for his taxes. I'm just saying . . . it's not like they're luxury cars. Maybe he's being more protective than indulgent."

"Okay. Fair enough. Either way, it's not typical."

"It's certainly not."

"Other things we know . . ." Merrick says. "The car was found locked with most or all of Randa's things in it—didn't look like anything was stolen."

"It had some strange things in it, which we'll get to in a minute," Daniel says, "but we need to ask what it means that it was found locked, with no signs of foul play and nothing appearing to be missing."

"Her phone was missing," Merrick says.

"Which we presume was on her person—probably in her pocket or maybe even her hand."

"But her purse and wallet, some cash, and jewelry were still inside."

"How much cash?" Daniel asks.

"Over a hundred bucks."

"We know from receipts and even surveillance footage that Randa went to an ATM and withdrew most of the cash from her checking account before she left Pensacola."

"Which was a little over four hundred dollars."

"And we know she stopped at a few places along the way and bought gas and food and some other items."

"About a hundred dollars' worth of stuff," Merrick says, "so where's the other two hundred bucks?"'

"In her pocket instead of her purse," Daniel says.

"Maybe. It's yet another question, another mystery. It doesn't appear to be a robbery but money is missing."

"Everywhere you turn . . . there are unanswered questions. Some of them small and specific . . . but others strange and inexplicable."

"Let's talk about what was in Randa's car," Merrick says. "And let's start with the books. Randa left most of her books back in her dorm room at UWF, so it's interesting which ones she took."

"I know we're going to get to this on a later show," Daniel says, "but I just want to mention now that most of the things in Randa's room were boxed up—something people who are going to commit suicide often do so loved ones won't have to do it. But, and this is a *very big but*, her stuff could've still been boxed up from returning from the holiday break."

"But that's not something you normally do, is it?" Merrick says. "Pack up all your stuff between fall and spring semesters. During summer, maybe, but not Christmas break."

"No, not usually."

"And we'll get into that in a future episode," Merrick says, "a very interesting episode, but for today let's talk about the books she brought with her—*Girl, Interrupted*, *A Bright Red Scream: Self-Mutilation and the Language of Pain*, a Bible, *The Virgin Suicides*, and *The Bell Jar* by Sylvia Plath."

"These books paint a certain picture," Daniel says. "A bleak picture of a young woman undergoing a breakdown or feeling like she might be. And I'm not saying you can diagnose a person by what they read, but . . . the fact that these are all books of a certain kind, of teenage girls in crisis . . . I don't think it's unreasonable to surmise Randa Raffield was not in a good way."

"Which leads to a couple of other items in the car," Merrick says. "A length of water hose cut just long enough to fit from the exhaust pipe around to the window, and a roll of duct tape."

"Was Randa Raffield suicidal?" Daniel asks. "And if she did kill herself out there—in the swamp or the bay—why wasn't her body ever found?"

"And why is there so much evidence to indicate she was abducted and murdered," Merrick says. "Next time, on *In Search of Randa Raffield*."

Chapter Eleven

"You think we can clear it?" Reggie asks.

"I do," I say.

We are in the evidence closet, pulling the material from the Randa Raffield case—all of which fit in a single cardboard storage box.

When I open the box and see how little is inside, I say, "Maybe I spoke too soon."

"Not much, is it?"

I carry the box to her office where the case files are waiting for us.

They are in a large black three-ring binder, which I place on the evidence box on the chair beside me across from her desk.

Rather than sitting behind her desk, she leans against the front edge of it, crossing her Roper boots.

"You sure about this?" she says, lifting a bottle of cold coffee from her desk and taking a sip.

"Absolutely," I say. "I'm already obsessed with it."

"Then I want you working it full-time," she says. "Put the Remington James thing on the back burner and give me the Robin Wilson case back. I'm gonna see if FDLE will take it."

"You wouldn't rather us investigate it?"

She shrugs. "I'll look at it again and let you know."

I nod and she takes another swig of her cold mocha coffee drink.

Her phone rings and she puts her coffee down and steps around the desk to answer it. As she does, I lift the binder and begin to flip through it.

Glancing over the file lets me know what a solid job Merrick and Daniel have done in handling the details of the case on their show, and I wonder if Reggie let Merrick look at it.

There's not a lot in the binder—a few reports, some statements, notes, and photographs.

Most of the pictures of the car are from the holding lot where it was towed—where it had been for two days. The pictures of the scene where Randa had vanished were mostly of the highway, shoulder, and surrounding woods—and were mostly useless.

Reggie finishes her call and looks up at me. "Lot of attention on this case. We need to tread carefully and protect our investigation. You and I are the only ones to see the file. I'm not sharing any info with Merrick or anyone else. I'm happy his podcast is doing so well. And I appreciate anything they've turned up, but it's a one-way street. They share with us. We don't share with them. It's our case. Let's solve it."

I nod. "Yes, ma'am."

"Let me know what you need. I'll do anything I can to help. Any resources. Anything I can come up with. And you can drop that *ma'am* shit."

I smile. "What happened to Randa's car?"

"Processed for prints, DNA, etc. Photo-graphed. Released to the dad. Title was in his name. From what I gather, he's kept it just the way it was in hopes she's still gonna show up someday, so if we need to take another look at it we might be able to—though what good it would do after all this time I can't imagine."

I nod.

"I looked through the case files," she says. "Been listening to Merrick's show. I think it's pretty obvious what happened."

"What's that?"

"Did you know Randa was an athlete?"

I nod.

"A world-class swimmer," she says. "On the swim team at UWF. Whether it was intentional or not I don't know—'cause I'm not a mind reader—but I bet you anything, she drowned. She walked into the woods and through the Windmark construction site and wound up in the water. Maybe she was just trying to sober up, maybe she really was suicidal. Either way, I think the most likely scenario is that she drowned. But we can't prove a negative. We need some evi-dence—anything that will prove to reasonable people what really happened."

"And if she didn't drown?" I ask.

"Then find the evil son of a bitch who took her and take him off the board."

Chapter Twelve

When I leave the sheriff's department, I intend to drive to my office, which is in the investigations division behind the supervisor of elections office on Long Avenue. The investigations division and interview room are in a separate location because the small sheriff's department offices behind the courthouse just doesn't have room for us.

As soon as I'm in my car, I begin the next episode of the podcast.

"Today we're joined by private investigator Cal Beckner," Merrick says. "Welcome."

"Thanks for having me."

"We appreciate you being on the show," Daniel says.

"Happy to help. I've invested a lot in this case over the years—and not just time."

"How'd you first get involved in the case?" Merrick asks.

"I was hired by Randa's mom, Lynn Raffield, oh I'd say . . . sometime in the second week of Randa going missing."

"So you've been on the case since nearly the beginning," Daniel says.

"Near about."

"Are you still investigating the case now?" Merrick asks.

"I am. And I will be until it's solved."

"But you no longer work for the family, is that right?"

"That's correct. I haven't in a long time. I'm working this case pro bono because . . . well, I . . . just can't let it go."

"And why did Lynn Raffield let you go?" Merrick asks.

"You'd have to ask her to be absolutely certain, but . . . my guess is . . . she didn't like what was in my reports and—"

"You focused on Randa's background, right?" Daniel asks.

"I did. Usually the keys to understanding something like this—a young girl not where she's supposed to be and winding up vanishing—are in the days and months and, to a lesser extent, years leading up to it."

"And what did you find in Randa's past?"

"A very troubled young woman," Cal says. "Randa was by all accounts a sweet girl . . . pretty genuinely nice to everyone. A good and loyal friend. A good student. Good athlete. But she was . . . she struggled too."

"With?" Daniel asks.

"Some drugs, but mostly alcohol. Binge drinking. Lots of parties."

"Which is pretty common on college campuses these days, isn't it?" Merrick says.

"Yes, it is. But I'd say Randa's was even more excessive than the typical excessiveness found among most coeds these days."

"There was a fair amount of alcohol found in her car at the time of her disappearance," Daniel adds. "Now, none of it was open and most of it was in the trunk, so we're not saying Randa was drinking and driving. We just don't know. But . . . she had enough booze for a party."

When I reach my office I keep driving, taking a right on 98. At the next light I take a left and drive down past the marina to park in front of the bay. Leaving the podcast running, I open the binder and begin to go over the case files page by page, picture by picture as I listen.

"Lynn Raffield, Randa's mom, didn't seem too surprised by her daughter's drinking," Cal says. "I think she knew about it or suspected. It was the other things I uncovered that I think led to her dismissing me."

"Which were?" Merrick says.

"Some of it's related to her drinking, but . . . some of it was . . . showed some . . . deeper issues and problems."

"Like?" Daniel asks.

"Promiscuity."

"Again," Merrick says, "something pretty common on college campuses."

"Not like this," Cal says. "Randa had a boyfriend. Actually, as of New Year's Eve of the year she went missing, a fiancé. Yet she continued to sleep around."

"Should we say allegedly or something?" Daniel asks.

"I have evidence," Cal says. "Now listen, I'm not trying to smear Randa or make anyone think differently of her. I like her. I really do. I uncovered so many good things about her. She was a sweet and kind person. But I'm sharing some of the things that I feel could've contributed to what ultimately happened to her. Which was what I was hired to do, and what I've continued doing all these years because I want her found. I want this mystery solved. I want this case closed. I want Jerry and Lynn and all Randa's friends to have closure. And what I'm saying is . . . Randa wasn't just promiscuous. She had a problem that went beyond that. She suffered from a condition, a compulsion. She was a sex addict."

"A sex addict," Daniel says.

"Yes. Someone who engages in a compulsive behavior, in this case sex, in spite of the negative consequences and harmful effects."

"And you're saying Randa did that?"

"The night she said yes to her boyfriend's proposal of marriage, she slept with another guy."

I look up from the binder and out at the bay. If what he's saying is true, it means her boyfriend is a bigger suspect than was first believed. So are the other people she was sleeping with—and their jealous partners.

"I don't say this lightly," Cal says. "And I wouldn't say it if I didn't have the evidence to back it up. This is a very serious condition and it makes me feel so bad for this sweet young girl."

"Okay," Daniel says. "Wow. I . . . I wasn't expecting that. But . . . if it's true, it could certainly have contributed to what happened to Randa."

"It's true. I have witness statements. Medical records."

"Medical records?" Merrick asks.

"From the number of sexually transmitted diseases and abortions she had. I've also got statements from some of her partners, her friends, and even the school records where her swim coach was fired over his alleged affair with her. Again, I'm not saying any of this to make Randa look bad. Just the opposite. I think we should all feel bad for her. She was a special, unique, strong, smart young woman with some very serious issues. She was also a cutter."

I think about the books and other items found in Randa's car and the picture of the damaged and faulty young woman in crisis it painted.

"Let me say it again," Cal says. "I think the world of Randa Raffield. She was beautiful. She was smart. She did very well at everything she did—made great grades and set records in swimming competitions. She was politically active. Socially aware. She was kind to people. A genuinely good person. But . . . beneath the outward perfection, she had some issues—issues that weren't obvious or even visible, but they were very real and were having a big impact on her life, and I think contributed to what happened to her."

"In what way?" Merrick asks.

"I think she was where she was because of these issues. She wasn't where she was supposed to be. Why? She was getting away from something. Could've just been the pressure of her life . . . but it could've been a stalker—someone she slept with who became obsessed with her. Maybe she really did intend to kill herself. Maybe that's why she was out there. And maybe she even did it. Or maybe she encountered someone who did it for her. Maybe she didn't resist. I don't know. We may never know what happened to Randa, but I hope we do—and not just to satisfy some morbid curiosity . . . but for her. For her."

Chapter Thirteen

"Merrick and Daniel's show really needs some female perspective," Anna says. "I appreciate what they're doing, but the show I just listened to had three middle-aged men talking about the mental state of a young woman."

"I had the same thought," I say.

It's early afternoon and I'm on Highway 98 in Panama City, heading west toward Seaside to see Jerry Raffield.

"NSSI is done as much or more by well-accomplished and high-achieving young women as it is by troubled, fringe, falling-apart young women."

"NSSI?" I ask.

"Non-suicidal self-injury," she says. "The cutting they were discussing. Some studies say as many as one in five girls between age ten and eighteen do it. It's not about suicide. It's not for attention. Most keep it a secret, do it where their clothes hide it. It's a release, a rush, a way to exercise control, and gives a sense of euphoria—just like the compulsive sex would. It's all about the brain, how it's wired, its biochemistry. It's about need and reward and punishment. I'm not surprised a high-achieving student-athlete like Randa did it—especially if she was as outwardly perfect and inwardly troubled as the private detective and others have indicated. Cutting, compulsive sex, perfectionism among these poor young women is like anorexia of the soul."

"How do you know so much about it?"

"I've been interested in it as it relates to women's issues a long time. Also from helping my niece with some of it a few years back."

"Our daughters are lucky to have you for a mom," I say.

"We're gonna have to be so careful with them," she says. "They're gonna get so much fucked-up pressure from our fucked-up sexist culture, so many horrible messages about every aspect of their bodies and beings."

"They're getting the right messages from us," I say.

"But the assumptions and . . . expectations and . . . conventions of an entire society . . . It's a lot to overcome."

"We're up to the task," I say. "Besides . . . our daughters have the best example imaginable in you."

"I worry about them," she says. "For them."

"I know, but . . . don't waste time on worry. And make sure you're not putting undo pressure or perfectionism on your parenting."

"I am," she says. "*See?* It's so . . . subtle and . . . insidious."

"Yes, it is," I say, and we fall silent a moment.

I can tell she's thinking, figuring, processing.

"Speaking of subtle . . ." she says. "Don't just take that PI's word that Randa was a sex addict or a cutter or whatever else he's saying."

"I won't," I say. "I talked to him this morning. He's agreed to give me copies of his files. Says they back up everything he said."

"Even if they do, or seem to, it may be wrong—or his conclusions may be, but even they aren't, they're still only a small fraction of who she was, of her story."

"Absolutely."

"She sounds pretty extraordinary from what I've read," she says.

"We've gotten a lot of emails and tweets and messages about our last show," Daniel is saying. "Specifically, how sort of creepy it is that two men, and in the case of our last show, three, are talking about a young woman's mental state, what she might have been thinking or why she might have done certain things."

"Yes," Merrick says, "and we've heard you. We didn't mean to be as obtuse as we seemed."

"And early on we did have on one of Randa's friends from UWF," Daniel adds, "and . . . the thing is . . . we've invited a lot of other women on the show . . . and gotten a lot of no's."

"And the show is new," Merrick says. "We're just getting started."

"Yes. But . . . we realize now we shouldn't just be two guys talking about a young woman and her mysterious disappearance."

"By far the most compelling and convincing argument was made by Nancy Drury on her *Nancy Drury Woman Detective* blog," Merrick says.

"Nancy expressed what so many were," Daniel says, "but did it in a masterful way. She's a good writer and thinker. She didn't trash us. Just laid out her argument . . . respectfully and . . . like I said . . . masterfully."

"So we asked Nancy to join us on the show today. Welcome Nancy. Nice to have you."

"Thanks for having me on," she says.

"I have to say," Daniel says, "I see Merrick and myself as pretty sensitive, aware, non-sexist guys, but until we started getting all the messages . . . it didn't really occur to me how stupid we were being."

"It was an epic fail on our part," Merrick says, "but one we're planning to remedy right now. Because . . . we've asked Nancy to be a regular contributor to our show. Sometimes she'll be on the show, but she'll always be in the background having input and keeping an eye on what we're doing."

"We should say that Nancy is an accomplished true crime blogger and podcaster herself," Daniel says, "and even did a whole show dedicated to the Randa Raffield case a while back. Why don't we start with you telling us a little about yourself, Nancy."

"Okay. Well, I have a background in communications and I've always been interested in true crime, real-life mysteries, and the criminal justice system, but it wasn't until it personally hit home that I began to blog about it. My husband was the victim of a hit-and-run. I started all this as a way to deal with that and search for the person who effectively ended his life. He's a quadriplegic who requires near constant care with no quality of life at all."

"Oh my God," Daniel says. "We're so sorry to hear that."

"Thank you. It happened quite a while ago and we've adjusted to a new way of life. I haven't found out who hit him, but working on it has led me to many other unsolved cases. It's staggering and disheartening how many unsolved cases there are out there. It's why I appreciate what you guys are doing. When I wrote what I did, I was doing so out of love for your show and the desire for it to be even better. I hope I wasn't overcritical and I certainly wasn't looking to . . . join the show."

"We had to beg her," Merrick says.

"Nancy has a lot on her and is doing this as a favor to us and as a gift to Randa and her family," Daniel says. "And we appreciate her so much for doing it."

"And you weren't overcritical at all on your blog about us," Merrick says. "Obviously, we needed to hear it. We needed a female perspective."

"And now we have it," Daniel says.

"It's important to say that I don't speak for women," Nancy says. "I don't speak for Randa. I don't speak for women in general. I can't. I can only speak from my perspective, which happens to be a female of a certain age who has been touched by tragedy and true crime."

"Well said," Daniel says. "You're making our show better already."

"Some would say it couldn't have gotten any worse," Merrick says.

The two men laugh, but Nancy, who clearly knows that Merrick is joking, takes the opportunity again to say what a fine job they've been doing.

"So before we move on today," Merrick says, "Nancy, is there anything you wanted to address that was said on our last show?"

"I'm sure we'll cover most of it as we move forward," she says, "but . . . just that . . . the pressures on young women in the world are enormous. Sometimes to the point of being crushing. And however Randa dealt with them or whatever she did to cope is far more complicated than we can begin to understand. Randa, like all of us, was an extremely complex human being. Being a human being is difficult enough, but being a female human being . . . It's like the quote about Ginger Rogers. Fred Astaire was great, but she did everything he did—except backward and in heels."

Chapter Fourteen

Seaside, the unincorporated master-planned com-munity west of Panama City along scenic 30A, is part of New Florida. Pottersville, Wewahitchka, and other small Panhandle towns are part of Old Florida. Certain cities—Tallahassee, Pensacola, Jacksonville, Panama City—have pockets of both Old and New Florida.

I'm part of and partial to Old Florida.

I have a love-hate relationship with most of New Florida.

The homes along the various master-planned communities of 30A are stylish in a uniform way, but are far too expensive for most Floridians and nearly all natives. They are the second homes and exclusive va-cation getaways of the wealthiest of Atlanta, Nashville, Birmingham.

Seaside was one of the first planned communi-ties to be designed using the principals of new urban-ism and includes the look of an updated old beach town with wooden cottages—though there's nothing old about it. The small town became world-famous when the Jim Carrey movie *The Truman Show* was filmed there.

Everything in this picture-perfect postcard of a small seaside town is soft and bright pastel colors of wooden beach cottages with tin roofs, framed mostly in white, surrounded by white wooden picket fences, pergolas, and gazebos.

The homes, which show the influence of Victorian and Carpenter Gothic and the antebellum South, all have small native yards and front porches filled with wooden Adirondack chairs, and are connected by a web of sand trail footpaths.

Among the many things to recommend Seaside are the incredible independent bookstore, Sundog Books, and the record store above it, Central Square Records—both of which I hope to visit before I leave if I can.

Jerry Raffield is one of the few native Floridians who can afford to live in Seaside and chooses to.

He's a roundish, laid-back, soft-spoken man with short curly hair, deeply tanned, heavily lined skin, small, sad blue eyes, and a smoker's voice—though there's no evidence on him or in his house that he smokes.

We are in his study—a beachy modern book room and office where he meets with his counseling clients.

"Thank you for coming, Detective Jordan," he says. "I really appreciate it."

The sound of his voice and the rhythm of his phrasing is hypnotic, and I get the sense that he is very good at what he does.

"Is there news?" he asks. "About my daughter, I mean. Have you finally found her?"

"No sir. I'm sorry, but I am here because we're devoting more resources to finding her. We have a new sheriff and she's assigned the case to me. I'm looking at it with fresh eyes . . . There's a lot of public interest in the case, lots of amateur detectives working it right now. Hopefully additional evidence will turn up and . . . ."

"I've always been . . . surprised by the . . . attention Randa's disappearance has received from the public. I'm not sure exactly . . . but my suspicion is that it's not a net gain for us. But if any of the . . . bloggers or podcasters or . . . turn up anything that helps us find her . . . I'll gladly amend my view."

The room is filled with pictures—on his desk, on the walls, on the shelves—of Randa frozen in time, never aging past a certain point, the beneficent bloom of youth bright upon her smile-crinkled face.

"You've had a lot of time to think about Randa's disappearance now," I say. "Has anything occurred to you that maybe didn't at the time you were first interviewed?"

"Lots, I'm sure," he says. "I'll have to think about it."

"Would you mind starting by just telling me about your daughter?" I say.

His small eyes glisten and he clears his throat.

"She . . . was . . . a . . . rare combination of tough and kind. She wasn't a soft sentimentalist but she'd do anything she could to help alleviate the suffering of others—often with some of the very things she herself was suffering from."

"Can you give me an example?"

He nods. "Sure. Randa suffered from PTSD. She led a PTSD group on campus. She knew what it was like to deal with the noonday demon of depression and even experience the desire for self-harm and . . . she volunteered at a suicide prevention hotline. But she wasn't just involved in the personal. She was political too. She participated in protests against the Iraq war. In fact . . . she was meant to be at one the night she went missing."

"Any idea why she wasn't?" I ask. "Or where she might have been headed?"

He shakes his head. "Second only to her disappearance itself, I find that the most bewildering. I just can't imagine what she was doing, where she was going."

"You said she suffered from PTSD," I say. "What . . . brought that on?"

"Her mom's drug-addicted, narcissistic sister has had a parade of bad men in and out of her bed and life over the years. But back then . . . we didn't realize just how bad she was, and she had been with the same guy for several years. We didn't find out until much later—long after he was gone—but he . . . repeatedly sexually assaulted Randa when she was a little girl. We were so ignorant of what was going on. They were our neighbors and they babysat for us all the time. He told her if she ever told anyone, he'd kill us. Told her how he'd do it in vivid detail. He took this sweet, kind, innocent child . . . and violated and brutalized her . . . When we found out, we got her medical and psychological care and treatment, of course, but the damage was done. I . . . I . . . didn't protect her . . . my little girl . . . my angel. I . . . bought a gun. The first one I ever owned in my life. I searched for him. I was . . . going to . . . kill him. I swear to God I was. But I could never find him."

It explains so much about Randa—the obsession and control, the cutting and sexually acting out.

"I'm so sorry," I say.

"Yeah, well . . . maybe you can find him."

"What's his name?"

"He went by Bill," he says. "Bill Lee, but . . . that wasn't his real name."

I write his name down in my pad and nod. "I'll find him."

"God, I wish you would."

"I will."

He nods and looks away, his gaze coming to rest on a picture of Randa hanging on the wall behind his desk.

"She was so . . . such a good, strong person . . . in spite of what happened to her. She was damaged, wounded . . . but she never gave up—on getting better or having the life she wanted."

He begins to cry softly.

"It's been almost twelve years," he says. "It could be twenty or fifty or a hundred . . . You never get over the death of a child. Never. I will never get over the . . . her absence in my life, in the world."

"What . . . do you think happened to her?" I ask.

"I think for a lot of reasons . . . she just got . . . it all got to be too much for her to . . . that she finally had enough and . . . did what she had to do to stop the . . . all of it."

Chapter Fifteen

The soft white sand leads down to the glasslike green Gulf, beyond which the horizon is a patchy modern painting of pastel pink, orange, and purple.

The tranquil beach at sunset is mostly empty, mostly quiet, completely transcendent.

"I think my daughter committed suicide and I think it's my fault," Jerry says.

We are looking at the beach from his backyard, which is so close as to be part of it.

Not far down from us the rooftop bar of Bud and Alley's, the restaurant named after Seaside's founder's dog and the restaurant's owner's cat, is loud with laughter, conversation, drinking, and people generally having a good time.

I wonder if it's difficult for Jerry to live here in this picturesque place of perpetual vacation. How dissonant the idyllic surroundings of paradise must be to a broken, sad, guilt-ridden, daughterless father.

"Why do you say that?" I ask.

"Something new I was trying at the time," he says, still gazing out at the sun sinking into the Gulf. "Tough love. I was taking a new approach with her. Confronting her about some of her risky behaviors, saying *no* to some of her requests, insisting that she get back in counseling. I think I pushed too hard. Or changed too abruptly. I think I drove her to . . . whatever she was doing, whatever she ultimately did."

If she killed herself, where is the body?

I make a mental note to ask Reggie about us organizing another search of Panther Swamp.

"You really think your attempts at helping her pushed her over the edge?" I ask. "Was she that close to the edge to begin with?"

He shrugs. "Obviously I didn't think so."

"If you step back and look at it as a psychologist and not a father," I say, "do you reach the same conclusion?"

He still doesn't look away from the western horizon, just wipes tears from his eyes.

"Not sure. Probably not."

If I am able to find out what happened to Randa, depending on what that is exactly, the burden of Jerry's guilt might be lifted a bit.

We are quiet a while.

"And you can't think of anywhere she might have been headed?" I ask. "Family member or friend who lives down that way—or even as far as Apalach, Carrabelle, or Tallahassee?"

He shakes his head.

"Maybe somewhere she read about, some place y'all vacationed when she was a kid."

"I've thought and thought," he says, continuing to shake his head. "Just can't come up with anything."

"What if she didn't harm herself," I say, "what if a very bad man didn't happen by just at the right moment, what would you think happened to her?

Would she have run away? Vanished to restart her life somewhere in anonymity?"

"I don't think so," he says, looking at me again. "She didn't really have a flight response, only fight. And I really, really don't think she'd do that to her mom or me."

"Then what?" I ask. "If she didn't harm herself, if she didn't intentionally disappear on her own, and if she wasn't happened upon by a killer of some sort, then what?"

"I always liked her boyfriend," he says. "Thought he was . . . extremely patient and understanding with Randa."

"Yeah?"

"But . . . I don't know . . . things have come out since she . . . disappeared. I don't know . . . I'm . . . I've been rethinking some things about him."

"We'll definitely be looking at him again," I say.

"He proposed on New Year's Eve at a big event in Pensacola. Local news captured it. I'm sure you've seen it. Every time her case is reported on, they show that same clip over and over. She said yes at the time, but one of her friends said it was just to keep from causing a scene or embarrassing him, that she had no intention of marrying him. What if she told him shortly before she went missing? Or what if he found out about the other guys she was sleeping with? I don't know. I'm not trying to point the finger at him. I know what that's like. So many crazies online say I killed her. Or me and her mom, that we're secretly still together, but live separately to throw everyone off the scent of our murderous guilt. There's been . . . so much craziness . . . I don't want to add to it, but . . . you asked what else might have happened to her. I wouldn't say this to anybody else—not the media or friends and family. Just the police."

I nod. "I understand. Thanks."

We are quiet again as the day turns to dusk.

"I wanted to ask you about the life insurance policy on Randa and what happened with petitioning the court to declare her dead."

He shakes his head. "What an unbelievable mess. There are people online who think I killed my daughter for insurance money. They say us having a policy on her is suspicious, but . . . my nephew was new in the insurance business and we bought policies for all three of us. It was as simple and innocent as that. They were set up as automatic withdrawals from one of our old accounts. I had forgotten we even had it. I didn't want the damn money. And I wasn't going to declare my daughter dead. We either find her or she's still alive to me, or the hope of her being alive is—at least in some small way. Lynn, my ex-wife, and I don't really talk, but I'm sure she feels the same way. It was her nutjob, narcissistic sister whose actions led to Randa being so traumatized in the first place who petitioned the court. She's always borrowing money from Lynn—or was. She thought she was going to get her hands on that money, but . . . after she did what she did, Lynn cut her off for good. Hasn't spoken to her since, as far as I know. Lynn and I both agreed to put up every dime of the insurance money as a reward for whoever finds our Randa."

Chapter Sixteen

When I get home I find Anna on our back porch, glass of wine in hand, listening to the night, looking at the moon and the stars.

Her face lights up when she sees me—and then again when she sees the bags in my hand.

"You brought me something from Sundog?" she says.

"*And* Central Square Records."

"You coming home to me was gift enough. This is like Christmas."

I hand her the bags and she tears into them while I pull up one of the old wooden Adirondack chairs and sit down beside her.

She holds up J. D. Vance's *Hillbilly Elegy: A Memoir of a Family and Culture in Crisis*. "I've been wanting to read this. Thank you so much."

"Figured you might read it to us while we're in the car together chasing down leads on this case."

"I'd love to."

"Our friend at Sundog says it's in the same vein as *Deer Hunting with Jesus* and will explain many of the dynamics of the election."

"It will be a nice break from the shit I'm encountering online," she says. "You should see what the evil little internet trolls write about Randa, her family, her boyfriend, her friends, even Merrick and Daniel and the other bloggers and podcasters. It's vile. Makes you lose what little faith in humanity you have left."

I frown and shake my head.

"They say the most outlandish and outrageous things, trash people's entire lives—with not a single shred of evidence. It's just crazy thoughts they have, random bullshit ideas with no basis in fact or reality—and they post it with impunity, with no regard for civility or decency or reality."

"That's the catchphrase of the moment, isn't it? We're living in a post-facts, post-truth world."

She shakes her head and looks as sad as I've seen her lately. "It's the very worst parts of humanity, and it's not just tolerated, it's celebrated. And there's so much of it. How can so many people be batshit crazy?"

"I don't have an answer for that, but to quote my favorite Midwest folk poet Mr. John Mellencamp, 'to say that we're doomed is just an obvious remark, it don't make you right just keeps you in the dark.'"

"Do you really think we are?" she asks.

"Doomed? No. I don't. Well, I guess sometimes I do. And in some ways we are. But for every narcissistic, egotistical politician, for every racist and sexist and bigot, and for every sad little internet troll, there are decent people doing good. Doesn't get as much attention or coverage, isn't as flashy or reacted to, but the good is there, quietly relieving suffering, continually making the world a better place."

"You give me hope, John Jordan," she says.

"You give me hope, Anna Rodden," I say.

Saying her last name reminds me we have to pick a date and plan a wedding.

"Love conquers all," she says.

"Only if she's allowed to," I say. "She works by invitation only. Love is simultaneously the weakest and strongest force in the universe. Now, open your other gift so we can give some expression to this great love we have."

She smiles and opens the Central Square Records bag. And squeals when she sees it's *Boz Scaggs Hits!* on the old original Columbia Records vinyl.

"You found it," she says. "We have to dance to our song right now."

"Yes, we do."

I stand and take her hand and lead her back into our living room.

As she turns off all the lights but a small one in the kitchen, I pull the old record out of its sleeve, place it on our new turntable, and find the very first song we ever danced to in junior high.

By the time the keyboard begins the familiar refrain, we are in each other's arms in the middle of our dark living room. By the time the strings begin, we are slow dancing like we did that first time. By the time Boz Scaggs begins to sing "Look What You've Done to Me," we are transported back to the commons area of Potter High School on a cool fall night following a home football game, when the world was still new to us and the possibilities it presented seemed to open up in an infinite and incomprehensible expanse.

"Best first dance song ever," she whispers.

I nod and thank God again for this gift.

Our bodies conform to each other's contours as we turn rhythmically round and round like the earth spinning beneath us, our own gravitational force pulling us toward each other as it has our entire lives.

And the mad world of American politics and true crime internet trolls and everything else that is inane and insane dims and fades away, and for this present, perfect moment there is only us, only love.

Chapter Seventeen

Over the next few days, I become even more obsessed with Randa Raffield, her life, her disappearance.

I continue to work the case.

Each night I go to bed with Merrick and Daniel in my ear feeding my obsession. Each morning I wake up thinking about it.

I attempt to set up interviews with Roger Lamott and Randa's mom and boyfriend, but meet with resistance and delays.

I meet with Reggie. She approves a new search and we organize and train volunteers to search Panther Swamp for Randa's remains.

Anna uncovers more and more information online—some of it useful, much of it not—all of it instructive.

We help Daniel and Sam move into a friend's empty unit at Barefoot Cottages, and Merrick and Daniel convert the guest room into their podcast studio.

Johanna comes for the weekend. Having her here with us makes our family complete, and I want her here all the time. Taking her back to her mom is extremely difficult for me to do.

Dad is undergoing treatment for chronic lymphocytic leukemia, and I'm both taking him to his treatments and trying to spend as much time with him as I can in between working two jobs and being with Anna and the girls.

Chris, Anna's ex-husband, continues to create and cause problems for us—or attempts to. At best, he's a severe irritant, like a stone stuck in the passageway of our lives. At worst, he's a spreading, incurable disease. And all of this is just a precursor of what's to come.

On the following Monday morning I drive out to the place on 98 where Randa's car was found, now the base of operations for the new search taking place.

Among the many volunteers, I discover Jerry Raffield. He's giving a short speech before the workers return to the woods.

"My family and I can't thank you enough for what you're doing," he's saying. "More than anything in this world, we want Randa returned safely to us . . . but . . . if that's not possible at this point, we want to know where she is and what happened to her. Now, I know you good people aren't doing it for this reason, but . . . there is a substantial reward for the person who finds her, so . . ."

Local TV stations have news crews videoing his speech. Nearby local newspaper reporters take notes.

When he's finished with his remarks, the reporters gather around him and ask a series of questions, which he patiently answers. He then looks directly into the cameras and makes a tearful plea—first to Randa to come home, then to whoever took her for mercy, then to the public for information to help locate her.

While he's talking to the media, I step over and speak to Gary Adams, the deputy organizing and overseeing the search operation.

He's a middle-aged thick black man with huge hands, a big head, and a quiet, no-nonsense manner.

"How's it going?" I ask.

"Wasn't expecting all the reporters," he says with a frown, "but . . . maybe it'll help. We got a pretty good turnout. More older people than I'd like. The thought of them traipsing through the swamp makes my sphincter pucker, but . . . we'll use what we've got."

I nod.

"I've told 'em if they find anything not to touch it, but you know they will," he says. "Trying to use the various emergency services folk we have to keep a close eye on the citizen volunteers, but . . . it ain't gonna be easy."

"I appreciate all you're doing."

"I took some special training on this and have a consultant friend I don't mind asking for help," he says. "She out here . . . we gonna find her."

"I have no doubt."

"'Course . . . she out here . . . she . . . bones. So . . . not tellin' the public, but we got cadaver dogs coming in later in the week."

I nod. "Thanks again. Let me know if I can do anything to help."

As I finish with Gary, a reporter for the Port St. Joe paper the *Star* approaches me. She is a young Hispanic woman who looks to be barely out of her teens. My guess is she's an intern still in college or this is her first job after graduating.

"I'm Sofia Garcia," she says. "With the *Star*. Can I speak to you for a minute? You're the lead investigator on the Randa Raffield case, right? What can you tell me about why this renewed interest in it? Is it because of the popularity of the *In Search of Randa Raffield* podcast?"

"Sheriff Summers encourages her department to continually pull out older case files and go through them with fresh eyes, keeping in mind recent DNA and other forensic advances."

"Isn't her boyfriend the one doing the show? Did he talk her into reopening the case?"

"There are a lot of citizens looking into this case," I say. "And we hope they may discover information that will help us—we always need the public to contact us with information, it's how cases are solved—but, and this is very important to remember, the official investigation into the case by the Gulf County Sheriff's Department is not connected with or influenced by any outside, amateur, or private investigations."

She presses—like any good young journalist should, but that's all I give her, and eventually she moves on.

When Jerry is finished with his interviews, he steps over to where I am, not far from the search command center tent.

"Hello, John. How are you? Thank you so much for all you're doing to help find my Randa."

"I was surprised to see you here today," I say.

"I've come out here searching so many times," he says. "I couldn't let others volunteer to do it without me being here to help, support, and appreciate them."

I nod. "How'd you even hear about it?"

He shrugs. "Not sure. Guess it was from one of the news stations wanting a comment or interview. Well, I better get out there and join in the search . . . I just wanted to thank you again for all you're doing. I feel more hopeful about finding her than I have in a very long time."

Chapter Eighteen

While everyone is searching on the north side of the street toward Panther Swamp, I walk across the highway and look around on the south side.

Walking along the soft, sandy shoulder of the road, I make my way over to the entrance of Windmark Beach, the St. Joe Company's coastal resort community on St. Joseph Bay.

Had Randa come this way? It's possible.

Windmark Beach is still largely a ghost town, its marketplace and community buildings mostly empty, the majority of its lots still vacant, but in 2005 when Randa disappeared there was even less. Far less. Mostly construction.

I pull out my phone and call Anna.

"Could you see if you can find out what was in Windmark in January of 2005?" I ask. "What was already built. What was under construction."

"Sure. Are you there now? I can go ahead and do it."

"If you can. If not, just when you can."

"I'll do it now and text you any pictures I can find."

"Thank you. Love you."

"Love you more," she says, and is gone.

I walk along Windmark's narrow paved road, under the decorative water tower, past the empty storefronts on the right and community buildings on the left, to the wooden bridge leading down to the beach.

Had Randa made this same walk? I could see her doing it, being drawn to the water.

I pause on the wooden bridge over the dunes and look back at the houses to my right. How many were here? Was anyone living in them at the time? Did anyone see her? Did her killer live in one?

When I reach the end of the wooden walkway, I'm reminded again of how narrow the beach is here. The thin strip of sugary sand is boarded by sea oat–covered dunes on one side and the bay on the other, its dark water expanding out toward the point of Cape San Blas and the greater Gulf beyond.

It's quiet and peaceful here—and would be even if it weren't early morning. The nearly four miles of beach lining this part of the bay is nearly always empty, appearing abandoned just like the resort community encroaching on it.

Looking out across the bay toward the Cape beyond, I wonder if Randa made the difficult but do-able, for her, swim and wound up over there. Had all the searches during all this time been looking for her in the wrong place?

My phone vibrates and I pull it out of my pocket. It's a text from Anna.

Wasn't much there at the time. Here are a few pics. Thank you. Love you.

LYM.

In another moment, three images of this area around early 2005 come through.

The thing that strikes me most about all of them is how raw and unfinished much of the property appears and how much construction was taking place.

Two nearby houses were in various stages of completion in early 2005. I walk over to them.

The structures are enormous, the architecture impressive, the lot the homes are on and the land surrounding them appearing natural and native, North Florida rustic.

I knock on the front door of the first home.

A trim middle-aged man with closely cropped, coarse salt-and-pepper hair, a deeply tanned face, bright white teeth, and light gray eyes opens the door and invites me in before he even knows who I am.

Declining his invitation to enter, I show him my badge and tell him why I'm here.

He shakes my hand enthusiastically, as if he's happy to meet me, his hand hard, his grip firm, and tells me his name is Bert Stewart.

"Were you living here at the time?" I ask.

He shakes his head. "House wasn't quite finished, not in January of 2005. I'd come down occasionally and crash when I was working on it—or, more accurately, overseeing the work being done on it, but we didn't move in until March or April of that year."

"Were you here the night of January twentieth?"

He shakes his head and shrugs. "I'm . . . just not sure. And I really don't know how I could go back and find out. It's so long ago."

"It was the day of George W. Bush's second inauguration."

"Oh. Well . . . Oh, yeah, I remember that. I was here, but didn't get in until late. The reason I came was . . . they poured my neighbor's foundation and my driveway the next day. I got a great deal on the concrete since they were coming anyway."

I turn to look at his driveway.

"Actually, it wasn't . . . my driveway was already here. It was . . . see that little pad on the side where I park my boat? It was mostly just that."

I nod. "Which neighbor? Right next door?"

"No that house was already up—was just a little behind mine. No, it was the one on the other side of that. Same architect and contractor did all three."

"What time did you get here that night? Did you see anyone else around? Do you remember seeing a young woman? Auburn hair. Pale white skin. Green eyes."

He seems to think about it. "It was pretty late. Not sure exactly. Maybe eleven. I . . . I didn't see anyone else . . . but . . . one of the . . . I saw a contractor's van parked a little ways down. It stood out because I didn't see anyone working and I didn't recognize the name of the company. Next morning when I got up . . . van was gone. Wow. Haven't thought of that . . . since back then. Not sure why I did."

"You ever see that van again?"

He shakes his head. "I guess I just figured our contractor had subbed something out to him, but . . . only subconsciously. I never really thought about it again."

"Your neighbor next door home?" I ask.

"She's not, but . . . she's new. Only bought the place and moved in about a year ago."

"And you didn't see a young woman that night, the night of the twentieth?"

He shakes his head. "Wish I had. Wish I could be more helpful. Sorry."

"What about the house one over, the one that poured the foundation at the same time you poured the pad for your boat? They home?"

He nods. "That's British Bob," he says. "What everybody calls him 'cause he's Kentish. He also goes by English Bob and Bob's Your Uncle. He's been here the whole time too. Got a great place. People have tried to buy it, but . . . he won't sell."

"Was he here that night?" I ask.

"I don't think so. If he was I didn't see him. Don't know why he would be. Didn't even have so much as a foundation at that point. But who knows? Bob's odd. That's what they should call him—Odd Bob."

"How so?"

He hesitates a moment.

"How's he odd?" I say.

"More . . . eccentric . . . I guess I mean. Maybe it's because he's British. Maybe it's because he's a life-long bachelor. I don't know."

I thank him, give him my card, and walk two doors down.

Bert had been right and wrong.

British Bob or Odd Bob or Bachelor Bob has an awe-inspiring place—even when compared to the other big, breathtaking homes surrounding it—but he isn't home.

So I pull out another one of my cards, scribble a note on it, leave it on his door, and—Bob's your uncle—maybe he'll call me back.

Chapter Nineteen

"Randa was not suicidal," Ashley Gaines is saying. "I keep hearing people say that—that she was out there to commit suicide. It's just not true. I keep hearing people say all kinds of shit. None of it's true. I knew Randa—and not just in general, but at the time she disappeared."

It's the following afternoon and I'm listening to more episodes of the *In Search of Randa Raffield* podcast as I drive in to Panama City.

"That's right," Daniel says. "There's a big difference in knowing or thinking you know someone way back versus when they went missing."

"People change," Merrick says. "Circumstances change. Situations change. How a person is feeling or what they're thinking changes. What do you think, Nancy?"

"Ashley is making a good point," Nancy Drury says. "Random people theorizing about Randa's state of mind in the abstract is worth exactly nothing. Ashley, what else can you tell us about Randa?"

"I'm not saying everything was seashells and balloons in her life," Ashley says. "She had problems to deal with like everybody else. She had her own issues too. But she wasn't suicidal. She didn't drive off to go kill herself."

"Why do you think she left?" Nancy asks. "Why do you think she was where she was instead of the protest in Atlanta?"

"I honestly don't know," she says. "And unlike other people who didn't even know her, I'm not gonna make shit up. I really don't get why she was where she was. I can't explain it—can't even . . . I have a hard time believing it. It's truly a mystery to me. I keep thinkin' maybe someone forced her to go there."

"You mean . . ." Merrick says. "You think someone could've been in the car with her, perhaps with a gun or something, making her do what she did?"

"I don't know. I have no proof of anything like that. And I realize after I said it that I'm doing what I just said I wouldn't do, but . . . All I'm saying is . . . it's so . . . out of character . . . I'm just trying to figure out how it's even possible. Randa was very responsible. She was a leader. In class. On the swim team. At work. She didn't do flaky shit. She just didn't."

Nancy says, "Some have suggested she was going to meet someone. What do you think of that explanation?"

"I . . . could see that. I guess. It'd be . . . Either she was going to help someone—she did that a lot. Maybe someone she knew needed her help. If so, I wish they'd come forward and say so. But I could see that. The other thing . . . I could see is . . . her . . . maybe . . . meeting . . . a . . . you know . . . guy. If

Randa was going to do something a little crazy or . . . you know . . . flaky, it would be for a guy."

"But she had a boyfriend," Daniel says. "Just got engaged. She had a fiancé. She'd just said yes a few weeks before."

"Well . . . the truth is . . . she said yes in front of everyone . . . didn't want to embarrass him—or herself—but later told him she didn't want to marry him."

"Really?" Daniel says.

"I'm pretty sure this is the first time anyone ever said anything like this," Merrick says. "I don't think anyone knew this before."

"I did," Ashley says.

"No, I mean law enforcement. Even people like us investigating the case. The media. The general public. This is huge. And . . . the implications are . . ."

"If investigators had known this," Daniel says, "they would've taken a much closer look at Josh Douglas, the guy everyone thought was her fiancé, and his alibi."

"No wonder he won't talk to anyone about Randa or her disappearance," Merrick says.

"Ashley, did Randa's other friends know?" Nancy asks. "Do you know of anyone else she told or who knew about it?"

"Yeah, I mean . . . I'd have to think about it, but . . . I wasn't the only one she told."

"Did she give the ring back?" Nancy asks.

"That's a good . . . I'm not sure. I don't know."

After they thank Ashley and she disconnects the call, there's a moment of silence.

"Did we just . . ." Daniel begins. "Did we just uncover something big? Something law enforcement didn't know?"

"I think we did," Merrick says.

"Oh my God," Daniel says.

You can hear the genuine thrill in both men's voices.

"That's something to savor," Merrick says. "Don't get many of those moments. I can tell you that."

"Nancy?" Daniel asks. "You still with us? Isn't it . . . incredible?"

"That's what we have to find out," she says. "How credible is it? Did Randa tell others about it? Did she give the ring back? We certainly need more corroboration. I have no reason to doubt that Ashley knows what she's talking about, but we've got to doubt or at least question everything. If it's true, others will know about it. And . . . on the other . . . the truth is we don't know what law enforcement knows. They may have known this and still cleared Josh as a suspect. We just don't know."

"You're right," Daniel says. "We've got to . . . verify everything—everything we can. It was just so . . . such a surprising and . . . potentially huge . . . piece of information or evidence . . . I got excited and jumped ahead and—"

"I'm not trying to be a downer," she says. "I think it's potentially . . . huge. Like you say. But we just don't know for sure if it's even true and if it is what it means."

"No, you're exactly right," Merrick says. "And we're so glad you're here."

"Even if I am a negative Nancy?"

"You're not," Daniel says. "Not at all."

"You're doing what we should have," Merrick says. "We lost ourselves for a minute. But if we don't question and doubt and most of all verify and corroborate, we'll be just like all the other assholes online with baseless speculation and ignorant, worthless opinions."

"Thank you, Nancy," Daniel says.

"No, thank you guys," she says. "I appreciate just how . . . open and . . . You guys really want to get at the truth and you put your egos aside to do it. It's very, very rare. I'm honored to be a part of your show."

Chapter Twenty

"What do you teach?" I ask.
"Political science mostly," Josh Douglas says.

He is standing at the front of his classroom unpacking his briefcase, placing books, papers, folders, a computer, and a bottle of water on his table and lectern, arranging them carefully as if following an exact plan long since committed to memory.

"I've always been drawn to politics. Randa and I both were . . . though . . ."

After repeated calls to Randa's fiancé going unreturned, I decided to show up at his classroom at Gulf Coast State College in Panama City to confront him in person.

The main campus of GCSC is crammed in the junction between Panama City and Panama City Beach where Highway 98 and 23rd Street intersect near the Hathaway Bridge and not far from Thomas Drive.

"Though what?"
He shrugs. "I don't know."

He stops what he's doing and we sit in two of the students' chairs at the table closest to the one holding his lectern, briefcase, and papers.

The classroom is plain—white walls, blue commercial carpet, two rows of tables with chairs beneath them, two dry-erase boards in the front, and a single bulletin board in the back, a few political news clippings tacked to it.

"I've thought so many things since she went missing, looked at everything a thousand different ways. There was so much I didn't know. Anyway . . . I've wondered for a while now if she . . . was ever really into politics or . . . just doing it because I did."

On my way into his classroom, I had asked a student out in the hallway to keep everyone out until I finished talking to him. Now, students periodically look at us through the narrow strip of glass in the closed door.

"You think she was faking?"

"Didn't at the time. Now . . . I don't know. And that's . . . the kind of thing that'll drive you crazy. Eventually, I figured out I had to just stop thinking about it. So I did. Mostly."

I nod and think about it.

"Just hope you never have to second-guess an entire relationship," he adds.

I know what he means, but think how often and for how many different reasons relationships get second-guessed—divorce, death, disappearance, breakups, even some that don't end. I've performed relationship autopsies on nearly every one I've ever been in.

He seems perfectly willing to talk to me and I wonder why he hasn't returned my calls.

"There's so much information out there," he says. "Sometimes . . . I have no idea who they're talking about. I just know it's not Randa. Others . . . I think I'm the biggest fool who ever lived and that I never knew her at all."

Josh Douglas is now thirty-three years old and bears little resemblance to the recently-old-enough-to-drink boy in the fading photographs with Randa. He's heavier, his body and face filled out, his blond hair darker and already beginning to thin, and he has a full, neatly trimmed beard.

I notice a wedding ring on his finger and realize that how I've been thinking about him, as Randa's fiancé, is wrong. He hasn't been that for a very long time—and maybe never really was.

"How long have you been married?" I ask.

"Six, almost seven years," he says. "Two kids. Alison, my wife, is . . . well, let's just say I needed a very special, stable, secure woman after what I went through with . . . Randa. She's great."

"What did you go through with Randa?" I ask.

He looks at me like I just asked him how to breathe and if it was really necessary.

"I don't mean her going missing or all that you've questioned since then," I say. "I mean before."

"Oh," he says, and gives me a nervous little smile as he lets out a sigh. "Randa was so beautiful, fun and funny, smart, and really caring. But she was . . . damaged too. Had . . . I don't know . . . I guess . . . some . . . childhood trauma. She required a lot—a lot of reassurance, attention, care . . . handling."

"She was needy?" I ask.

He nods. "Not always, just sometimes, but when she was, she really was—we're talking . . . a lot."

"Was she ever unfaithful?"

His eyes widen and he swallows hard. He then frowns and nods slowly. "I didn't realize just how much until later. Much later. But I knew she had . . . sexual issues. Knew that's how she got most of her reassurance and sense of worthiness."

"How did you handle that?"

"Like the classic helper-healer-savior I was trying to be," he says. "It wasn't easy, but . . . I'd always worked through it and doubled down on my commitment to her. She was always so scared I was going to abandon her."

"Were you ever unfaithful to her?" I ask.

"Never. Not once. Even thought of only her when I'd masturbate. It was crazy. Extreme. Tried so hard to prove my love to her, to prove to her she was worthy of it. You ever tried to convince an extremely insecure person you love them and won't leave them? It's impossible. But like Sisyphus, I woke up every morning to push that boulder up that hill."

"Did she sleep with any of your friends or people you knew?"

He nods. "She slept with everyone. And not just the guys. Girls too."

"What made you propose when you did?"

"Thought the Pelican Drop would be memorable as hell and—going back to my earlier answer—to try to reassure her, to try to make it work. Pushing that boulder."

"She said yes?"

"She said yes in the moment, but didn't mean it. Or . . . hell . . . she may have meant it at the time. But not long after she told me she didn't want to marry me, that she couldn't. Said I was too weak. Said she needed to be with a stronger, more powerful and dominant man to keep her ass in line."

"How'd that make you feel?"

"You know the answer to that, but the horrible fuckin' feelin' didn't last long. Soon enough I felt free. Like I had dodged a bullet. And even from the very beginning, I felt grateful she didn't embarrass me in front of all those people at New Year's. That was good of her."

A student trying to see in the door bumps into it and Josh turns toward it, then glances at his watch. "I've got to start my class. I'm already late."

"Just a couple more quick questions. Where were you the night she went missing?"

"Where she was supposed to be—the war protest in Atlanta. I didn't know she wasn't coming until I got a call from her on the bus when we were about to leave. I had called her several times. She finally called me back . . . but only to say she wasn't coming."

"Did she say why?"

"Family emergency, she said, but I could tell she was lying. I knew a little better by then."

"What'd you think it was?"

"Figured she was meeting someone. We saw each other even after she said she couldn't marry me. Not as much. Far more casual. Far more as friends. But when she called that day, I told her I didn't even want to do that anymore. I ended it with her right then and there and . . . have always felt guilty. Wondered if I caused her to do what she did, if I . . . could have been responsible for what happened. Maybe if I hadn't done what I did, she . . . wouldn't have been where she was and . . . wouldn't have wound up . . . dead."

"How do you think she died?" I ask.

"I have no idea. None."

"I mean by her own hand or someone else's."

"Oh. I don't know. She was such a . . . mystery. Sometimes . . . she was so different. It . . . it really depends on which Randa she was that night. But my guess is . . . someone got her. I know she felt like killing herself sometimes. She even talked about it occasionally, but . . . I don't know, I think it was mostly just talk. I think it far more likely she met the wrong man or randomly ran into him. 'Course it might not have been random at all. He could've been following her."

Something about the way he says this last line makes me think it might be an activity he's had some experience with.

Chapter Twenty-one

"Tonight we're joined by Toby Collins of the *Barstool Detective* podcast," Daniel says.

"Toby has a popular true crime podcast," Merrick says. "Unlike ours, where we take one case and work it for an entire season—or until it's solved—Toby does a new case every three episodes."

I'm driving home from Gulf Coast State College, making my way through Panama City toward Highway 22. It's dusk and all the taillights and headlights are a little brighter before the backdrop of evening.

"But that doesn't mean he isn't able to go in-depth," Daniel says. "He's known for digging deep into the cases he features."

"Right," Merrick says. "And that's why he's joining us here tonight—because of how deep he went into the time right before Randa went missing. Welcome, Toby."

"Good to be here. Thanks for having me. I've really been enjoying your show. You guys have always been interesting and . . . easy to listen to, but . . . adding Nancy was genius. In fact, one of the reasons I agreed to do your show tonight is to see if I might steal her away from you."

They laugh.

I only have a few more shows before I catch up to where the podcast is currently, then I'll have to wait a week between episodes like everyone else who's listening live. Of course, I hope we're able to close the case before very many more shows are made.

"That's very sweet, Toby," Nancy says. "Tell you what . . . as soon as we solve Randa's case we'll talk about it. How's that?"

"Well let me see what I can contribute to getting this thing solved."

"Toby has really delved into the events leading up to Randa's disappearance," Merrick says. "And some fascinating theories of why she was where she was and what may have happened to her."

"What do you think happened to Randa?" Nancy asks. "Just in case you were thinking about burying the lead."

"Well, obviously I don't know," he says. "Mine are just theories like everybody else's, but I try to tie them all to actual, provable facts. So let's start there. Here's a fact: Randa's car had almost a full tank of gas in it when she went missing. And the doors were locked."

"And what conclusions do you draw from those facts?" Daniel asks.

"I know a lot of people do, but I don't believe Randa had any intention of harming herself. You don't fill up your car with gas if you plan to commit suicide. And she had to stop and fill it up pretty close to where she wrecked. So . . . you see . . . that's just an opinion . . . but it's tied to a fact. Now . . . it's entirely possible I'm misinterpreting the facts, but . . . there it is."

"What do you think her car being locked means?" Merrick asks.

"That she intended to come back to it."

"So you think she locked her car because she was planning to come back," Nancy says, "but then she met with foul play?"

"Or accidental death," he says.

"Just seems like we'd have found her remains by now," Nancy says. "Especially if she had met with an accident."

"I know—and that bothers me too. There are so many holes and unexplainable mysteries in this thing. We may never know what really happened. It's what makes it so interesting to me."

"So . . . we know Randa stopped for gas not long before she got in the wreck and went missing," Merrick says. "Do we know where? Do we know of any other stops she made?"

"We do," Toby says. "I was gonna start at the beginning and go chronologically, but why don't we do just the opposite. Since we already started with the car, let's work backward from it. She stopped at a Racetrack gas station on Tyndall Parkway and filled her car up. She went inside and used the restroom, but didn't purchase anything but the gas. The station is on the outskirts of Panama City on Highway 98, not far from Tyndall Air Force Base and about twenty-five miles from the scene of her accident."

"Is there surveillance footage?" Merrick asks.

"I believe so, but I haven't seen it. No one in the press or public has."

"That's so close to where she went missing," Nancy says. "I never knew it was that close. Someone could've seen her there and followed her—maybe even caused her wreck."

"Yeah," Daniel says. "That seems far more likely than a killer happening upon her at the scene."

"It's one of the theories that fits best to me," Toby says.

"Wouldn't you like to have the files and evidence the police has?" Nancy says. "I feel like we could solve it if we did. I'd love to see the surveillance footage and . . . well, everything."

"Gulf County Sheriff's Department doesn't inspire confidence," Toby says. "That's for sure."

"Well, it was very different back then," Merrick says. "It's a new department. New sheriff. New lead detective."

"That's right," Toby says, "you have a connection to the sheriff. I forgot. Sorry."

"I'm just saying I bet they reopen the case, and if they do I'm betting they'll have different results."

"I sincerely hope so," Toby says. "Okay, backtracking further back, we know Randa stopped in Destin to get food and go to the bathroom. This is based on receipts and witness accounts. As far as I understand there is no surveillance footage. Before that, before leaving Pensacola, we know she went to an ATM not far from the UWF campus and took all but two dollars out of her checking account—a sum of about four hundred and twenty dollars. And I understand there is surveillance footage of that."

"What time of day did she leave?" Daniel asks.

"That's interesting," Toby says. "She packed her car and left campus pretty early that morning according to witnesses in her dorm. And her ATM withdrawal was early too—before eight. And the receipt from the restaurant in Destin is around eleven. So if she wrecked her car at almost ten that night . . . that means it took her—"

"Eight extra hours," Nancy says. "Where was she? What happened in all that time?"

"My guess is we'll never know," Toby says.

Chapter Twenty-two

"Exactly," Toby says. "Did she break down somewhere else? Meet someone? Take a detour? What?"

"That's a lot of missing time," Merrick says.

"Here's another thing," Toby says. "She volunteered at a suicide hotline in Pensacola, but she had the night off because she was supposed to be traveling to participate in a protest in Atlanta that day. But . . . at some point during the day she disappeared, she called the supervisor and told her she'd be able to work after all because she wasn't going to the protest. But then she never showed up."

"That's so . . . strange," Daniel says.

"So we know she intended to be back for work that night," Nancy says.

"Unless that was a ruse of some sort," Toby says. "Some people believe she did several things like that because she didn't want people to know what she was really doing, didn't want to be found after she did it."

"Do we know why she backed out of the protest?" Nancy asks.

"She told the organizer that she had a family emergency to attend to," Toby says.

"And we know for sure she has no family near where she wrecked or farther in that direction?" Daniel asks.

"Never been able to find any. And a lot of people have looked. If she would've continued on the direction she was headed, she would have gone through Port St. Joe, Apalach, Eastpoint, Carabelle, and ultimately Tallahassee, passing the roads to Cape San Blas and St. George Island along the way."

"And all those places have been thoroughly checked?" Merrick asks.

"I believe so," Toby says, "but can't be certain. I know both of her parents and other family members who've been interviewed said she had no family in any of those places and they didn't know of any friends or acquaintances."

"Where the hell was she headed?" Nancy says.

"That *is* the question," Daniel says.

"One we don't have an answer to," Toby says. "Not yet, anyway."

"Now, Toby, you've said you believe Randa died by either accident or foul play, that she was most likely murdered. But there are facts that paint a different picture, evidence that could cause reasonable people to draw other conclusions, right?"

"Absolutely. We know Randa was a special person and that she always appeared to have everything together, but that she struggled with some depression. I think that's why she was drawn to the helpline. So I'm not saying it's impossible that she was on her way to hurt herself in some way—though why she was out there and where she was headed I can't imagine, if that be the case. Why not just do it in Pensacola or at least somewhere closer or some place that had significance to her?"

"For those who believe she wished herself harm," Daniel says, "what is the evidence? What do they point to?"

"Her history of depression, anxiety, and other issues," Toby says. "Most of which was never seen by even those close to her. Really took some digging to uncover. Her erratic behavior in the days leading up to her disappearance. The fact that she was out in this place so far from where she was supposed to be and no explanation can be found. And, most convincing of all, the fact that she had a piece of garden hose and a roll of duct tape in her backseat, and the hose was just the right length to reach from her tailpipe to just inside her window."

"That's all pretty compelling," Daniel says. "Am I wrong to say that, Nancy?"

"Not at all," she says. "We just have to remember that there may be other reasonable explanations for every single one of those things. It's very difficult to know what another person is thinking and it's very easy to reach the wrong conclusions when looking at things the wrong way from the outside."

"No question," he says. "We have to keep an open mind about everything and try to look at all of it from every imaginable side."

"True," Merrick says. "Now . . . Toby . . . something happened on campus, actually in Randa's dorm the day before she disappeared . . . that you and a lot of other people believe had a huge impact on her leaving and acting the way she did—and explains what she may have been doing out in the middle of no-where all alone. Can you tell us what that was?"

"A young woman named Chelsea Sylvester overdosed in Randa's dorm. It's not conclusive whether it was intentional or accidental, but she was a friend—or at least an acquaintance of Randa, and there was talk among the young women who lived in the dorm that Randa had something to do with it— either supplied her with the drugs, was there when she took them and/or took them with her, or even had some sort of suicide pact with her and this was how she followed through."

This is the first I'm hearing of this. There is nothing about it in the file, and I haven't heard anyone mention it.

I pause the podcast and call Reggie.

"Did you read the entire Randa Raffield file?"

"Yeah. Why?"

"Was there anything in it about a connection she may have had to a young woman who died in her dorm, Chelsea Sylvester?"

"No, nothing. Never heard of her—let alone a connection to Randa. Where'd you hear—"

I tell her about the podcast.

"I guess I need to start listening to the damn thing," she says. "I'll ask Merrick about it and call you back."

"Have you watched all the surveillance footage?"

"Yeah. Quality is low. Why?"

"Were you looking to see if someone was following her?"

"Sort of. I'm tellin' you . . . it's hard to see much of anything on the recordings."

"I'll watch them tonight."

"How'd you make out with the professor?" she asks.

I tell her. "Do you know if his alibi was ever verified?"

"No idea, but even if it was, we need to check it again."

"Probably gonna need some help chasing some of this down," I say.

"Sure. Whatever you need. Hell, I can do some of it myself."

Chapter Twenty-three

When Anna and I arrive at Sam and Daniel's new place in Barefoot Cottages with bags of groceries, we find Sam undergoing physical therapy and learn that Daniel, Merrick, and Nancy are upstairs in their new home studio recording another episode of *In Search of Randa Raffield*.

We tell the day nurse she can go ahead and leave, that we'll keep an eye on Sam until Daniel comes down.

When she is gone, I unpack the bags and put things away while Anna begins to make dinner.

The kitchen, dining nook, and living room all occupy one large open area. Sam's therapy is taking place on a massage table in the living room, so we are able to observe the work the therapist is doing with her while we make dinner.

The cottage is relatively small, with everything close together. A door off the living room leads to the master bed and bath, while on the opposite side a half bath beneath the stairs is also the laundry room.

The beachy decor gives it the feel of a vacation rental instead of a permanent home.

Sam's therapist, a short, trim, dark-haired, hairy man, is patient and kind but firm, and seems to be pushing her just the right amount.

I'm amazed at the progress she's making. And I'm not the only one.

"Sam, you're doing amazing," Anna says. "Your strength and determination are an inspiration."

Sam attempts to say something but what comes out is unintelligible.

She's a small woman—both short and petite—even smaller since her injury, with just shorter than shoulder-length blond hair, large blue eyes, and pale white skin. She's an agent with the Florida Department of Law Enforcement and was injured while we were working a case together.

The prognosis her doctors have given her for a complete recovery from the gunshot wound to the head she suffered isn't good, but her doctors don't know her the way we do. My money is on a full recovery—or at least enough of a recovery that she and I will work another case together one day.

When her therapy is over and she is exhausted, her therapist and I help her back into her bedroom and the hospital bed awaiting her there. Next to it is the single bed Daniel sleeps on—what little sleeping he does between checking on and caring for her.

When we have her situated, she looks up at me, gives me a partial smile, then shoots me with a thumb and forefinger gun.

I shoot her back with one of my own and our eyes lock for a long moment.

"Better save your bullets for the bad guys," I say. "We're gonna have some catching up to do once you're back in the saddle."

She nods intently and narrows her eyes.

By the time her therapist and I prepare to leave the room, she is fast asleep.

I leave the door open—not only so we can keep an eye on her but so she can be a part of what's going on out here.

The therapist leaves and I help Anna finish dinner. A short while later, Daniel, Merrick, and Nancy bound down the stairs excited about the show they've just recorded.

"I think that was our best yet," Merrick says.

It's obvious from his energy and bearing that he is the leader, the driving force behind the show.

"Me too," Nancy says.

"When do we get to hear it?" Anna asks.

"From the smell of that dinner you're cooking, anytime you want," Daniel says as he steps over and looks in on Sam.

Daniel and Merrick are around the same age—early forties—but Daniel is darker, quieter, more reserved.

"John, Anna, this is Nancy," Merrick says.

"Nice to meet you," she says.

Though she is taller and a little larger and about ten years younger, it's amazing how much Nancy resembles Sam. Similar blond hair and blue eyes.

"I feel like we already have," Anna says. "Love listening to you. Love what you bring to the show."

"Thank you. That's very sweet of you to say."

"Can you stay for dinner?" Daniel asks Nancy.

"You have to," Anna says.

"I'd love to but I need to get home to my husband. I've already stayed longer than I intended to."

"It's ready," Anna says. "What if we eat quickly?"

Nancy smiles. "That's so . . . sweet of you. Let me call the nurse and see how he's doing and how long she's willing to stay."

It occurs to me how similar a situation Nancy and Daniel are in, and I can certainly see how helpful it is for them to have the podcast as an outlet.

Nancy lives in East Point, on the other side of Apalachicola, about a forty-five-minute drive away, so even if we eat super quick it'll still be well over an hour before she's able to get back.

"What about Reggie?" Anna asks Merrick. "Can she join us?"

He shakes his head. "Afraid I've got to go too. We have a friend's birthday party tonight." He looks at me. "But I was hoping to talk to you about the case. Can we get together tomorrow or sometime soon?"

I nod. "Just give me a call and we'll figure out a time."

"Will do," he says. "Great show guys. See you both soon. Talk to you sooner. Anna, it's breaking my heart to leave such a good-smelling meal."

He leaves and we begin to set the table.

In another few moments, Nancy returns. "He's doing okay. She's willing to stay, but . . . I can't leave him much longer and I don't want you guys to rush for me."

"Sit," Anna says. "Eat with us. John's never eaten slowly in his life. You won't be rushing us at all."

Chapter Twenty-four

The four of us sit, serve our plates, and begin to eat.

Anna has made her famous spaghetti and meatballs, soft garlic-butter French bread, and salad. They all have red wine. I have water.

"You did it again," I say. "It's delicious."

She smiles at me and pats my hand.

"I made extra," she says to Daniel. "I'll make plates you can warm up this week."

"Thank you."

"You're welcome to take some too," she says to Nancy.

"I'd love to. It's so good. Thanks."

"I love the name of your podcast," Anna says. "Appreciate that you used *woman* instead of *girl*. Is Nancy Drury your real name?"

"Yeah, well, Nancy's my middle name, but yeah. Before the podcast I always went by Beth, but as many people call me Nancy as Beth these days."

"Sorry to say I haven't listened to your show yet," Anna says. "Trying to finish *In Search of Randa Raffield*, but as soon as I do . . ."

"Daniel and Merrick's show is much better than mine. I'm all over the place. Lots of different cases. Tend to ramble."

"It's a great show," Daniel says. "She doesn't ramble, doesn't . . . It's great. No other podcast comes close to being the victim advocate you are."

"Stop. You're embarrassing me."

"Okay, but it's true."

Daniel and Nancy are easy to talk to, and we have a nice, relaxed conversation that flows well. We each keep an eye on Sam, though no one more than Daniel, who actually goes in to check on her occasionally.

"So tell me about Chelsea Sylvester," I say. "I heard you guys talk about her on the show I listened to today. I'd never even heard of her."

"It's very sad," Nancy says.

"It's legit," Daniel says. "Suspicious death. Friend of Randa. Lived on the same floor. There's some question as to whether it was intentional or accidental, but . . . I say either way it would've had a big impact on Randa. She could've felt responsible, but even if she didn't . . . she would've been upset, shaken. It's probably why she cancelled everything, jumped in her car, and drove . . . toward her fate."

"Maybe she didn't just feel guilty," Nancy says. "Maybe she was. Maybe she killed her and then couldn't . . . kill herself. Maybe she didn't actually kill her . . . Maybe she provided the drugs. Maybe she knew they were bad."

"There's talk that they had a falling out," Daniel says. "There's a lot we didn't share on the show. More than one of their friends said Randa slept with Chelsea and that Chelsea broke up with her girlfriend, Brenda Young, in hopes of being with Randa."

"I think it has something to do with what ultimately happened to Randa," Nancy says. "Even if it was just what got her out here on the road that night, but . . . I really think it's more than that."

"Can't believe the original investigation didn't consider any of this," I say.

"The original investigation was lacking to say the least," Daniel says. "Some people online have posted how they think there's a conspiracy or cover-up or that the Gulf County Sheriff's Department is involved somehow, but . . . I just believe it was incompetence or more likely laziness."

"Another possibility is that Brenda killed Chelsea and Randa was running from her," Nancy says. "Pure speculation, but . . . we're not on the air. I think it's possible Brenda was stalking her—and could have even been following her that night and . . ."

Daniel's phone vibrates and he picks it up from where it sits facedown by his plate and looks at it.

He then gasps as his eyes widen and all the color drains from his face.

"What's wrong?" I ask.

He shakes his head as if trying to jar something loose. He then shakes his phone. "Come back," he says to it.

"What is it?" Nancy asks.

"The In Search of Randa Raffield Snapchat," he says. "Just got a snap or a chat from Randa Raffield."

"*What?*" she says.

"That's the name that came up on the screen. It was an old picture. Only lasted a second. But it was her. She was . . . it looked like she was about to be murdered. She was tied up to a table. A man with a knife was hunched over her. Can I get it back? How do I get it to come back?"

"You can't," Nancy says. "Unless . . . see if it'll let you replay it."

"It won't."

"If he sends it again, screenshot it."

"How?"

"Push the power and home buttons at the same time, but it's got to be quick. You only have a second."

"What is it?" I ask.

"Snapchat," Nancy says. "It's an app for mobile devices that lets you send pictures or videos that self-destruct after between one and ten seconds—depending on how you set it."

"So the picture was there for one second and now it's gone and we can't get it back?" I say.

"Right."

"How sure are you it was her?" Anna asks.

"Positive. But . . . it was an old picture. I'd say back from when she first went missing. Oh my God. It was . . . so . . ."

"I'm assuming Snapchat wasn't around back when Randa went missing," I say.

"No, it wasn't."

"So someone . . . probably her killer . . . set up an account in her name to taunt us," I say. "How hard would that be to do?"

"Not hard at all," Nancy says.

"Can we trace the account?" Anna says.

"I'll call Chris and see if he can help us," I say.

"And it was the podcast snapchat not your personal?" Anna asks.

"I don't have a personal. That's why we put the show one on my phone."

"May I take a look at it?" Nancy asks.

Daniel hands her his phone.

It starts ringing and she jumps. "Shit," she says. "Scared the shit out of me. Merrick's calling." She hands the phone back to Daniel.

"Hey," he says into the phone. "Yeah, we saw it too. Well, I did. Where'd . . . oh shit."

He pulls the phone away from his mouth and says to us, "He got the same pic on his personal account. He was driving and couldn't screenshot it."

I look at Nancy. "If he sent it to Merrick's personal account and not just the show's, he may have sent one to you too."

Her eyes widen and she grabs her phone.

"Maybe he'll send it again," Daniel is saying to Merrick. "Who do you think it is?"

"Shit," Nancy says. "Bastard. I have one too."

"Nancy got one too," Daniel tells Merrick.

"But . . . it's not on my personal account. It's on my *Nancy Drury Woman Detective* show account."

"Can you screenshot it?" Anna asks.

157

"I'm gonna try."

Chapter Twenty-five

Nancy holds her phone out in front of her, fingers in place.

"Wait," I say, getting up and moving over to stand behind her chair. "I want to be looking at it in case you're not able to save it."

"Wait," Anna says, jumping up and joining me. "I want to see it too."

"Okay," Nancy says. "Ready? Here . . . goes . . . nothing." She presses a button on the screen to open the image, then quickly starts pushing buttons on her phone.

The disturbing image is only on the screen for a second, but it's long enough for it to sear through my eyes and into my mind.

Randa is not only bound, but she's gagged, and true terror fills her green eyes.

"Oh my God," Anna says, placing her hand over her mouth.

"Did you get it?" Daniel asks.

She presses a few places on her screen and brings up a group of images. The most recent one is a screenshot not of the picture of Randa, but her Snapchat contacts background.

"Damnit," she says. "I missed it. Sorry."

I try to remember everything I can about the image.

Not much of the background was visible—and what was, was dim—but it looked to be a basement or garage or workshop of some kind. She was tied to a table or workbench, not a bed—there was no frame or headboard. Her face was damp with both sweat and tears. Duct tape held the gag in her mouth. The man leaning over her was average, but his knife was definitely above average—a long, wide serrated blade that gleamed even in the dimness.

"Weren't those . . ." I begin. "Her clothes. Isn't that what she was wearing the day she disappeared?"

"That's all I can picture now," Daniel says.

"Me too," Nancy says. "Don't know if that's what she had on or if I'm just projecting them onto her now. Sorry."

"Merrick says it is," Daniel says. "They are. That's what she was wearing."

"Wonder if he killed her right away and this is one of his trophies," Anna says.

"And with all the renewed interest in and added attention on the case," Nancy says, "he had to gloat, to interject himself into the case to make sure we know he did it."

I nod. "Best thing y'all could do is ignore it, not acknowledge it on your show."

"That has my vote," Daniel says. "This is freaking me out. Would it make me a total pussy to admit I'm a little scared to stay here by myself tonight?"

"I think the term you mean is *ball sack*," Nancy says. "They're very fragile and tender, whereas everyone knows a pussy can really take a pounding."

He laughs. "Point taken."

"I like this woman," Anna says.

"But no," Nancy says, "it doesn't make you a total ball sack. This is creepy, freaky shit."

"Merrick says it does," Daniel says.

"Remind him he's the one out there all alone in his car on that dark, empty road," Nancy says.

"Says he has a ball sack of steel," Daniel says, then to Merrick, "Okay. Sounds good. We'll talk tomorrow if any of us are still here." He disconnects the call. "He's gonna tell Reggie about it and let us know what she says."

"This is the most excitement I've had in a very, very long time," Nancy says, "and I really don't want to, but I have to go. I've already been away from Jeff a lot longer than I should've been."

"We'll follow you," Anna says.

"I'm fine," she says. "I'll be fine. Besides, you can't leave Daniel."

"I'll get a deputy to come over here and we'll follow you," I say.

"That's sweet, but not necessary. It's just a picture. Hell, it may be Photoshopped. Could be one of those nasty little trolls punkin' us. But even if it's Randa's actual killer . . . doesn't mean he's going to do anything to us."

"Let them follow you," Daniel says. "I'd feel a lot better about you going."

"John needs to work on this, not babysit me," she says. "I'll be fine."

"He can work on it when we get back," Anna says. "We insist."

"Just as long as you insist on leaving an armed deputy here when you go," Daniel says.

He's smiling and partially kidding, but only partially. He suffers from panic attacks—something being alone here with Sam after what's happened can't be good for.

Over the years, Daniel has consulted on some pretty high-profile ritual murder cases, and even helped Sam with a couple of her more challenging and brutal investigations—one in which a compulsive killer was using fire as a weapon and another that involved kidnapped conjoined twins. He had survived but not before a significant amount of damage had been done.

Daniel gives Nancy a hug. "I know you have your own escort and everything, but call or text when you're in safe and sound and let me know."

We follow Nancy in her small Rav 4 SUV along 98 out of Port St. Joe, into the woods of Franklin County that leads to Tate's Hell, through the old fishing village that is now a quaint, quiet tourist destination of Apalachicola, up on the high bridge over the bay, to her small wooden home in East Point.

"Thank y'all so much," she says as we get out of our vehicles. "I feel bad making you drive all this way."

"You didn't make us," Anna says. "We made you."

"Mind if I look around before we go?" I ask.

"Not at all," she says. "That's sweet. Let me just check on Jeff and let the nurse go. I know she's way past ready. She lives right there behind us. A few times she's actually left a few minutes before I got back."

I nod.

We don't have to wait long.

"Had she already gone?" Anna asks.

Nancy shakes her head. "But she didn't waste any time leaving once I walked in."

I search the house while she and Anna make us coffee and snacks in the little kitchen for our drive back.

The house is small and chopped up into little rooms the way all of them used to be. Two bedrooms, a living room with a fireplace, a dining room, a den, one bathroom, and a tiny kitchen in the back. Jeff is asleep on a hospital bed surrounded by various machines in the small front bedroom. Nancy's computer and podcast equipment is set up in the den.

Looking through this modest house and the modest life it holds for Nancy, I'm grateful again that she and Daniel have podcasting as a new outlet, and I hope we'll be able to close the case for them—as well as for Randa and her family. Of course, if we do, what will they do then?

After everyone is gone, Daniel's house is quiet again, and he returns to his lonely little life.

But tonight he's not just alone and lonely, he's frightened, and can feel a panic attack at his ragged edges, threatening to develop, to descend upon him like the merciless bird of prey it is.

He tries to distract himself by thinking about the podcast, the case, but that inevitably leads him to the horrific image on his phone and . . .

He can feel an attack coming on.

Heart pounding.

Head spinning.

Panic.

Pressure.

Fear.

Loss.

Stop. Breathe. Relax. You're okay.

He had lived in fear for so long, and then Sam came along and he had found his equilibrium, his calm. *She* had been his equilibrium, his calm. But now she's gone, she's living a kind of half-life where she's—

It's nowhere near half a life she's living.

Taking a deep breath, he attempts to slow the progress of the panic attack by thinking of what a badass Sam used to be—and how, with her, he was too for a little while.

She had fought the Phoenix and won. Together they had beaten the killer making burnt offerings of his victims. They had worked the Shelby Emma Summers case, not just looking but diving into the abyss, fighting monsters not fearlessly but relentlessly, never letting fear stop them.

Now look at them.

Sam is less than half alive. And he's less than half the man he was with her.

After wiping down the counters and putting away the last of the leftovers, he goes into what should be their bedroom, but is her home hospital room.

As he does, he pictures Nancy doing the same thing, living the same half-life as him.

Each evening, after the day is done and it's just the two of them again, he bathes and changes her. It's the closest thing to intimacy they experience, and though he finds it infuriatingly frustrating, he nonetheless looks forward to it.

He misses Sam so much he feels it physically, feels the deep, dull ache in every single cell of his body.

He studies her scars, tracing the tumescent tissue with his fingertips.

She is more scarred and more attractive than any woman he's ever seen. Her body is a beautiful poem of pain, of strength and healing and resiliency.

We are our scars, he thinks. Both seen and unseen. I am no less mine than she is hers.

With a soft, warm bath cloth he washes her scarred body, caressing every contour, making love to her with the basin and the towel, symbols the world over of love and service, acceptance and purification since Jesus first used them to wash his disciples' feet.

Except for the scars, the missing breasts, the paleness of her skin, her body still looks like that of a woman half her age, and he's so grateful the physical therapy is enabling her to keep much of her muscle tone. She's certainly lost some strength and athleticism, but she has plenty left to build on if she is able to recover to an extent where she might be active again.

But what are the chances of that really happening?

She's making gains, but they're so slight it seems inaccurate to call them progress.

He leans down and gently kisses her ear.

"I miss you," he whispers to her. "Please come back to me."

When he pulls back, she is looking up at him with sad eyes, and they both begin to cry.

Chapter Twenty-six

Anna and I are driving back home from Nancy's when Reggie calls.

"Whatta you think?" Reggie asks. "Is it him?"

"The killer?" I ask. "Or abductor or whatever he is?"

We're on the winding coastal section of 98 not far from East Point, Apalachicola Bay to our left, above it a big bright moon, orange earlier, now fading to bone as it rises higher in the night sky.

"Yeah."

"No idea," I say, "but I think there's a good chance it could be. Fits with a certain type of killer. But . . . that's the problem. Fits with a certain type of internet troll too."

"We really do battle with evil sometimes," she says. "More and more it seems like."

I don't say anything, just think about the truth of what she's saying.

"Did you see the news tonight?" she asks.

"No."

"You were on it," she says. "So was Jerry Raffield. It was at the search site. You were in the paper today in a story about the case that young reporter for the *Star* did."

"Sofia Garcia?"

"Yeah."

"Okay?" I say, wondering where she's going.

"Bet you anything you're next," she says.

"Next for—"

"To get a message."

"Not if he only uses Snapchat," I say. "I don't have an account."

"I'm serious," she says. "Bet he sends something to the dad too. Unless it *is* the dad."

"Well, if he does," I say, "it's more likely we're dealing with the killer."

"How do you figure?"

"Podcast goes everywhere," I say. "They have listeners all over the country, all around the world. The paper and the TV news are local. If he sees them, it's far more likely it's her killer and he's still in the area, not some maladjusted loner with a computer and internet connection in his basement in Wisconsin."

"Then I hope you hear from him."

"Me too."

"Be careful," she says. "I've got a bad feeling about this."

"Will do."

"Samantha Michaels is such a vivid reminder of how quickly something horrible can happen."

"She's gonna get better," I say, "and I'm gonna be fine."

"Let's make sure Merrick and Daniel are too."

"And Nancy," I say. "She's a target now too. We will. Speaking of . . . Could you ask the Franklin

County Sheriff to send deputies by to keep an eye on her place?"

"On it. See you in the morning."

Reggie was right.

When I arrive home and check my email, there's a message from ColdBlooded-Killer@gmail.com waiting on me.

I know you think you are smart, Mister Detective Chaplain John Jordan, but I am smarter. You think you are everything. You are really not much. You have only been up against lightweights before, but now you're in with a real heavyweight. Way over your head. You have never seen a cold-blooded ruthless son of a bitch like me. Be assured of that. Back off now or I will come for someone you love and like that pretty little auburn-haired girl, they will never be seen again. Think about it. There is nothing you can do to make Randa come back to life, but you can cause someone you love to lose their life. Is it worth it? For what? I do not want to see that happen. I am warning you because I do not want to do it. I really do not. But I will. I will do what I have to. And you should know that I can. I did not get away with this for twelve years without being brilliant and merciless. I will win. You cannot beat me. You will lose. Someone will die. And for what? For nothing.

"So . . ." Anna says, "he's local. Still in the area."

We are at the desk in my library looking at the computer together, waiting for Chris Andrews to arrive.

"Can't know for sure, but . . . I think he is. Got to figure out how to protect everyone. I'm sure Merrill and Dad and maybe even Jake will help us. We've got to figure out protection for Johanna in Atlanta. I think Reggie can handle protecting Merrick and their kids, but . . . I'm most concerned about Daniel and Sam and Nancy and Jeff."

Anna nods.

"Do you want me to stop?" I say.

"Would you?"

"Absolutely. No question. You and the girls are . . . everything. I'll walk away tonight if you tell me to."

She shakes her head, her eyes glistening. "Thank you, but . . . just keep us all safe—including yourself."

"I will."

"It means more to me than you'll ever know that you're willing to walk away for me, for us."

"It's not even a difficult decision," I say.

"But I know it's who you are, what you were created to do."

"Who I am is yours. I'm Taylor and Johanna's father. I'm your husband—or soon will be. We still need to pick a date and plan a wedding, by the way. I'm those things first and last. I'll stop being an investigator if you want me to. Right now. I'll call Reggie and resign right now."

"But you'd be unfulfilled, you'd . . . Don't you think you'd eventually resent me and the girls?"

"Absolutely not. No way."

She smiles and her eyes do that thing where they express nearly more love and appreciation than I can handle. "I believe you. I know what you're saying is true. Thank you."

She starts to cry, and I hug her.

"I lived with a self-centered man for so long," she says. "He always put himself before me, before everything and everyone. I . . . I just . . . I'm so grateful for you, John."

"I'm grateful for you, for what we have. Nothing else comes close. Nothing."

"I know. I . . . just . . . don't . . . know . . . how to handle that."

"You're handling it just fine," I say. "Now, let's get everyone protected and see if we can't track down who sent the picture and this email."

Chapter Twenty-seven

Chris Andrews is a small, soft-spoken man in his early forties with a clean-shaven head and face and blue eyes the color only contacts can create.

He was a few years behind me in high school but we were good friends even back then and have only grown closer since then.

He's an absolute computer genius, a hacker extraordinaire, which is how he makes his living, though I have no idea exactly what he does or how legal it is, but his real passion is performing. Before the Fiesta in downtown Panama City closed, he was the headliner of the drag show every weekend, his extravagant costumes, exquisite choreography, and impeccable impersonations receiving a standing ovation every single time.

He's seated at my desk, doing things never before done to my computer. I'm hovering behind him, looking on with bewilderment and awe.

"Not gonna find any naked pictures of you and Anna on here, am I?" he says.

I shake my head.

"Pity."

"Whatta you think?" I say. "Will you be able to track him?"

"Not sure yet—having just started and all . . . Jeez . . . I can tell you this—what he's done requires a pretty high level of sophistication. Our boy's no dummy."

Dad and Verna are staying here tonight. Dad is out in the living room with both his holstered sidearm and a shotgun. Merrill is at Sam and Daniel's similarly armed. Reggie has a deputy posted outside her house—and has Merrick and all their kids inside with them. Jake is set up in his truck outside Nancy and Jeff's place. And Frank Morgan, a retired GBI agent who helped me work the Atlanta Child Murders, is keeping an eye on my ex-wife Susan and our daughter, Johanna, at their home in Atlanta tonight.

"How's Doug?" I ask. "Thought you might bring him."

"He had rehearsals in Panama City tonight. Probably just getting home about now."

Doug, Chris's husband, is a talented African-American stage actor who does carpentry and contract work to pay the bills.

"Did I tell you we're doin' a show together?"

"Othello, right? When is it?"

Doug and Chris are working on a modern re-telling of Othello with Doug playing Othello and Chris playing Desdemona.

"We're raising funds now and hope to be able to stage it in January."

"Speaking of which," I say, "I got approval for you to get paid for the work you do for me. Sorry it took as long as it did."

"I'm doing it as a friend for you," he says. "Not for the sheriff's department or money."

"I know. And I appreciate it. You're still doing it for me. You're just getting paid for it. And it's about time."

"I like helping you," he says. "You've always been . . . so . . . good to me. Did you know back in high school you were the first person I came out to?"

"I guess I didn't," I say. "Not the first."

"You were. You were the only one I could even imagine trying to tell. And you were so . . . sweet, so supportive, such a good friend."

"Probably could've been better if I hadn't been so obsessed with the Atlanta Child Murders," I say.

He laughs.

"Chris, you don't owe me anything for acting like a decent human being back in high school," I say. "I hope you don't think you do. We're friends and I love you. Doug too. I'd do anything I could for you. You've always been the same way, but I never thought it was because you thought you owed me."

"I don't."

"Good. So you'll be paid for this and you'll put it toward the production and Anna and I will be there in the front row."

"Thank you, John."

"So now that you're making all this money, can you explain to me how someone can send a picture from a fake Snapchat account or an email message from a fake email account?"

He laughs. "There are sites online set up to help you send fake Snapchat messages. Or he could've just set up a fake account. Email is more difficult, but the real question is going to be whether we can trace the accounts."

He continues to work as he talks, clicking and typing, opening various windows and searching through them.

"Two basic ways to send an email from a fake account that can't be traced are to create a temporary email address from a site designed for that very thing. There are several. The problem is that they mostly wind up in the recipient's spam filter because the address is from an unknown, uncommon, or unusual domain. Like the fake Snapchat series that are supposedly benign, meant to be used to punk your friends, these sorts of temporary email addresses are supposedly meant for signing up for sites you don't want associated with your actual address. Of course, both can be used for ill—as in this case. Second option would be to sign up with a legitimate email provider through a proxy that wouldn't immediately get spammed. This will obfuscate your location from the email server and allow you to send emails that appear to be coming from pretty much anywhere you want. Looks like he used a pretty complicated combination of both of these tactics. It's gonna be very difficult to trace him. Maybe even impossible. He went to hella lot of trouble to make sure you wouldn't."

"That's what has me worried."

Chapter Twenty-eight

"Today we're joined by Dr. Arther Dyson," Merrick says. "He's a forensic psychologist—teaches and has a practice, and has done so for nearly thirty years now. Welcome to the show, Dr. Dyson."

"Happy to be here."

"We're thrilled to have you," Daniel says, "and can't tell you how excited we are to hear what you have to say and to share it with our listeners. And we need to thank Nancy for setting it up."

"Dr. Dyson was on my show a while back and I thought he'd be a real asset to this case."

I'm in my car driving into work the next morning, listening to the podcast and thinking about the case as I do.

"It's vital to remember that there are all sorts of murders and motives for murder," Dyson is saying. "Some murder is a direct result of psychosis—a murderer hears voices telling him to kill and he obeys. Some murder is sexually motivated. Other motives include revenge, domestic disturbances or so-called crimes of passion, those committed under the influence of drugs or alcohol, those committed to cover up another crime, greed, etc. But most murder is the result of situational, stressful factors. In fact, think about the very first murder ever recorded. It's a great pattern case for the typical murder. It's the story of Cain and Abel in the Bible, and it contains most of what you need to know about most typical murders. Cain killed his brother Abel—most murders involve a close relationship between offender and victim. He killed him out of jealousy—God liked Abel's offering better. It was a direct, violent assault. And when the killer is confronted with the murder, he lies. God asked Cain, Where is your brother, Abel, and Cain said, I know not. Am I my brother's keeper? Most of this type of murderer—people who kill a loved one, family member or friend—are captured fairly quickly. Other types—a stranger, serial killer, a psychotic in his own world—can take longer. But most murder victims aren't killed by strangers. They're killed by people they know. They're killed by people they're connected to, people they're closely, emotionally involved with."

"So you're saying it's more likely than not that Randa knew her killer?" Merrick says.

"Well, remember what I said about those kinds of killers—they're usually caught pretty quickly. Statistically, you're more likely to be murdered by someone you know, but . . . given the circumstances of your case . . . it could be the lower percentage killings done by a stranger, a serial killer, or an opportunistic killer. You know . . . it's not like there had to be a serial killer out trolling for victims at that exact location at that exact time that night. This could be situational. Maybe the murderer didn't plan on killing her, maybe something happened, things got out of hand . . . and . . . *bam*. Happens all the time."

"In cases like those," Nancy says, "are the victims' remains usually so difficult to find?"

"Depends, but most killers don't want to get caught. They'll go to great lengths to evade capture, and hiding—even destroying—the body is an important first step to doing that. And you have to remember . . . it's possible the body isn't all that particularly well hidden. Maybe it's just hidden where no one's looking. Maybe Randa climbed into a vehicle with someone who took her far, far away and killed and buried her body there. Could be anywhere. All it really has to be is where no one is looking."

Daniel says, "But if we stick with the higher probabilities, it's more likely than not that Randa knew her killer, but . . . if she did . . ."

"Okay, let's take that scenario for a moment. What if Randa was being followed by someone who was obsessed with her, a stalker. She wrecks. He comes to her aid. She confronts him—says what the hell are you doing way out here? He lashes out. Strikes her or . . . kills her in some way. Hides her body. Resumes his normal life. It's possible the police have even interviewed him, but nothing came of it . . . or maybe they even suspect him but have no evidence and he didn't rattle when they spoke to him."

"What if rather than stalking her," Nancy says, "someone was actually in the car with her. Maybe she was out here to meet someone or maybe the person came with her from Pensacola. They're drinking. They wreck. Lock the car and leave it to go sober up. And somewhere—on the beach, in the bay, in the swamp—something happens . . . and he kills her. Then leaves. Hikes. Walks. Gets a ride. Returns to his life without ever being suspected."

"It's possible," Dyson says. "It's all possible. And even though some of the scenarios are more probable than others . . . we just don't know enough to . . . It could be the least likely scenario imaginable. Could be a total stranger killing. She could've encountered a serial killer out there. Given that it's been almost twelve years and there's been no trace of her . . . I'd say . . . in this particular case . . . it might be more probable at this point."

I pause the podcast with enough time to call and check in on everyone before I reach the station.

"All quiet here," Merrill says. "Wish it wasn't. Love for the creepy fucker to show his ass around here."

"I understand the sentiment," I say, "but I'd much rather us figure out who he is and show up at his place instead of him coming to ours."

After I finish with Merrill I call Jake.

"Thanks again for doing this," I say.

"It ain't no problem. Got shit else to do right now."

"Well, I really appreciate it."

"I've been sitting here thinkin'," he says. "I've got the background, the training, the skills. Thinkin' about gettin' my private license. Do some security and investigation work. Whatta you think?"

"It's a great idea."

"Thing is . . . I been lost for a . . . well, since the election and losing my job. Doing this for y'all—you and this sweet lady . . . It's been a while since I've felt any kinda useful."

"Do it," I say. "Let me know how I can help. I'll send work your way when I can. How's everything down that way?"

"Sad," he says. "She's sweet and all but that's one sad lady with a sad little life. What happened to her husband?"

"Hit-and-run."

"*Fuck*. That's the crime you should be solving. Find the fucker who did that."

"We should, you're right. Though I think if he could be found Nancy would've already found him. But I'll ask her. See what we can find out."

"Just let me know what I can do to help," he says. "I'm all in."

Chapter Twenty-nine

"You okay?" I ask.

Reggie looks up at me from where she's staring, a worried expression on her face.

"Come in," she says. "Sorry. Was just thinking. How's it going? Everybody still safe?"

"Everybody's good. But you don't seem to be. What's going on?"

She shakes her head and frowns. "Letter to the editor," she says. "It was in the same issue you were in about the search for Randa. Calls me corrupt. Says I'm hindering the investigation into the previous sheriff and his deputies. Says I'm feeding Merrick information about the Randa Raffield case to help his ratings. And generally what a bad job I'm doing."

"Let me guess," I say. "From someone who wants your job."

She gives me a half smile. "Doesn't mean he's wrong. Not about the other, but . . . I . . . I may just not be cut out for this job. I knew going in . . . I wasn't a politician, but . . . I . . . I thought I might make a good . . . be good at the other . . . I don't know. Doesn't matter."

"You're a great sheriff," I say. "I wouldn't want to work for any other."

"Thanks, John."

"I'm serious. You're doing such a good job. Don't let some asshole who's trying to set up his campaign against you get you down."

"You just called someone an asshole," she says with a smile.

"Wanted you to know how serious I was," I say.

"You should run," she says.

"From what?"

"*For* sheriff."

I laugh. "They say to never say never, but that will *never* happen."

We are quiet a moment.

"I was insecure about taking the job to begin with," she says. "I'm still unsure about how I'm really doing. Most of the time I don't feel like I should be doing it at all. So when I'm criticized I . . . it just sends my insecurities into overdrive. I've come close to resigning so many times."

I nod my understanding. "I hope you won't. I understand how you feel, what you're saying, and I know me saying something different isn't going to change the way you feel, but . . . again . . . you're doing a fantastic job—and doing it backward in heels."

"Someday we'll talk about this more in depth. I'll share with you all the reasons why I feel like I'm not qualified, we'll evaluate my performance since I've been in the position . . . and we'll see if you feel the same way."

"I'm sure I will, but okay. Anytime you like. As far as the murder of the previous sheriff, I know

FDLE is investigating it, but why not let me look into it too? And announce that I am. And why not call a press conference about the Randa Raffield case, give an update, ask for tips and help from the public, and go on record about not supplying Merrick with information."

"Those are good ideas. I'll think about them. Do you know we don't even talk about the case anymore—not since we reopened it and you started working it—not at all."

"Probably best."

"Oh, and speaking of the case . . ." she says. "Got a call from Lynn Raffield's attorney. He said a lot but it all boiled down to the same thing—she's not willing to talk to us at this time."

"Really?" I say. "She's just flat out refusing?"

"Says it would be too upsetting for her. Says she's devastated by the loss of her daughter and just can't bear to talk about it. He went fishing by saying it'd be one thing if we had new leads and were close to making an arrest, but that if we didn't he saw no reason to subject his client to more pointless questions."

I shake my head and think about it.

"He did say if we wanted to submit questions to him, he'd see what he could do about getting her to answer them."

"Another fishing expedition," I say. "He wants to know what we know and what we don't. The questions will tell him."

"I thought the same thing," she says. "I find it all very suspicious."

We are quiet a beat, each of us sipping our drinks—her, steaming hot coffee, me, ice-cold Diet Cherry Coke.

"Any luck tracking the Snapchat pic or the email sent to you?" she asks.

I shake my head. "Doesn't look like we're going to be able to. Chris is going to try a few different things, but . . . doesn't look too promising. Merrick said you looked into some earlier threats they received. Anything come of that?"

"Not a damn thing. Seemed to just be idiots with too little life and too much time and internet access."

I nod and think about it. "Think this is different."

"I said I don't talk to Merrick about the case and I don't," she says, "but I do listen to the podcast now. And I had an idea. When they were talking about the theory of someone following or being with her . . . We know her dad still has the car."

I nod. "Still in storage. Waiting for her. Cranks it up occasionally, charges the battery. That's about it."

"What if someone was in the car with her," she says. "Shouldn't we have the FDLE process it? There could be hairs, fibers, or DNA from her passenger if someone was with her."

I nod. "I had the same idea," I say, "but . . . there were probably so many people in the car prior to that night. We know most everyone close to her will have been in it and left trace evidence, plus . . . we have no idea what all her dad has really done to it since he's had it. Eleven plus years is a long time. Mechanics, family members, who knows? We know he gets in it regularly to crank it."

"Yeah, you're right."

"Couldn't hurt to have it processed. Just might not help."

"Could hurt my budget—and for nothing if we're pretty sure we wouldn't get anything useful."

Chapter Thirty

"I can't say for sure he was," Sage Isaacson is saying.

Sage Isaacson is an early thirties African-American woman with honey-colored skin, long dark hair, and black eyes that light obviously loves.

We're talking to her via Skype on Reggie's computer in her office.

She was the young woman who organized the busload of UWF students to participate in the inauguration day protest of the Iraq War in Atlanta back in 2005 when Randa went missing.

I've just asked her if she remembers Josh Douglas being with them that day.

"You can't?" Reggie says.

We're Skyping with Sage because she now lives in Houston.

"Sorry, but . . . I just can't be absolutely certain he was there with us in Atlanta. It's been a very long time."

"Did y'all have a log or sign-in sheet of who went?" I ask.

She twists her lips as she seems to think about it. "I think so, but . . . again . . . I can't be positive. And I don't know if anyone would still have it."

Behind Sage is a huge, nice home—a big, open, expensively furnished living room with a large, modern kitchen with industrial stainless-steel appliances in the background.

"Obviously we're investigating what happened to Randa," I say. "So why don't you tell us what you do remember from that day that might relate to either her or Josh."

She takes a deep breath, frowns, and sighs. "This is not very PC of me to say, but . . . you know how in a group of some size there are a lot of different types of people and you can tell who's a chaser, a gold digger, a politician, a liar, a flake, you know like that. Well, Randa was a victim. You could tell, you know. She was sweet and pretty and smart and should have been . . . I don't know . . . more—more popular, more successful, more something, but she was . . . It seemed to me that she was or was going to be a victim. I guess what I'm saying is that I wasn't surprised when I heard something happened to her."

Reggie nods and says, "We appreciate your candor. We really do. Tell us anything that comes to mind. How did Randa let you know she had decided not to attend the protest?"

"She didn't. Just didn't show. I thought she might meet us there . . . maybe ride with Josh or— *wait*. That's right. When she didn't show . . . Josh got off the bus. Said he would drive up and meet us there, that he had to talk to her first. He . . . he was on the bus. We were getting ready to leave. He got a call. Then he suddenly got up and grabbed his things . . .

said he had to talk to Randa first but he'd definitely be at the protest, that he'd meet us there. Bring her if he could."

"Did you see him in Atlanta?" I ask. "Any-where at any time."

She puts her thinking expression on again, which soon fades into a frown. "No," she says, shaking her head, "I didn't. I don't think he was there."

"Who else could we ask?" Reggie says. "Who else might have seen him or would know if he wasn't there?"

"I can put together a list of people and their contact info. I've stayed in touch with some of them over the years."

"That would be great. Thank you."

A gray and white cat jumps up on the large marble-top island in the kitchen behind her, slinks over to a bowl, haunches down, and begins to eat.

"Anything else you can tell us about Randa or Josh or anything?" I say.

"I liked her. Felt bad for her—even after she slept with a guy I was talking to at the time. It was like I could tell she was damaged goods and didn't mean anything by it. Like . . . she couldn't help herself. A lot of people, mostly guys, were obsessed with her, wanted to save her, rescue her, take care of her."

"How did Josh handle that?" I ask.

"Like a saint. He was patient and understanding. Like he really got her deal and didn't take her acting out personally. It's interesting. He was obsessed with her too, but . . . just handled it so well. I don't know how he did it. I really don't. Anyway, hope that helps. Been a long time. I'm sure I'm forgetting a whole lot. I'll email you a list of some other students from back then you can talk to."

It's New Year's Eve. The streets of Downtown Pensacola are packed. The illuminated pelican is dropping.

Ten . . . nine . . . eight . . . seven . . .

The DJ is leading the crowd in the countdown.

The quality of the video footage from a local TV station is low, the camera whipping about, attempting to give viewers a glimpse of what it's like to be there.

six . . . five . . . four . . . three . . . two . . . one . . .

The pelican lands.

"Happy New Year everyone," the DJ says.

The camera moves about showing couples kissing, but when it gets to Randa and Josh it lingers.

"First question of 2005 goes to Josh Douglas," the DJ says.

He then walks up to where Josh and Randa are standing.

As the DJ extends the mic so Josh's question can he heard, Josh kneels down, hitting his head on the mic and making a loud thud, followed by feedback.

"Randa," Josh says, pulling the ring box out of his pocket as he takes a knee, "will you do me the honor of being my wife?"

The camera pans to Randa—along with all the eyes of those around them.

Randa looks taken aback, embarrassed, confused, angry, uncomfortable.

It's difficult to watch.

After a long, awkward moment, she nods.

"What was that?" the DJ asks, shoving the mic into her face.

"Yes," she says with no emotion.

Josh has to grab her hand and lift it so he can place the ring on it and the DJ has to tell them to kiss.

"Congratulations to Josh and Randa," he says. "May they have a long, happy life together."

I pause the DVD.

Reggie says, "It was nice of her not to reject him in front of all those people and on TV, but . . . anyone paying attention could tell that's what she was really doing."

We are still in her office, watching all the video and surveillance footage we have of Randa.

"No doubt. Poor guy."

"Poor guy should have been more clued in to what his girlfriend wanted and didn't want."

"True."

I start the disc again.

A series of still frame photos from the ATM Randa used at her bank near the UWF campus before she left Pensacola the day of her disappearance show her swiping her card, entering her pin, punching buttons, taking her cash and a few seconds later her receipt.

The quality of the images is very low, but they show Randa is alone and doesn't appear to be under any duress.

I jump back to the beginning and watch the images unfold again, this time looking only at the background.

"There," Reggie says, "look at that."

I pause the frame.

Someone is behind her. Not close. Maybe ten feet away. Randa is blocking our view of him. Only his shoes are visible—black Puma sneakers with Velcro flaps.

"Could just be someone waiting to use the ATM," I say.

"Probably is."

I start the disc again and we watch as the guy wearing the shoes stands there a little longer but then leaves before she finishes her transaction and turns around.

"That could be something," Reggie says. "He left before she turned around."

"Solid black Pumas with Velcro flaps," I say. "Could prove useful."

We watch the rest of the images but the shoes don't reappear and no one is visible when Randa turns and leaves.

The next footage is by far the worst quality. It is black-and-white exterior-only surveillance footage from the little mom-and-pop restaurant where Randa stopped to get food and use the restroom in Destin. She is only a black ghostly figure surrounded by grayness as she enters the front door of the establishment.

"Can't even tell that it's her," Reggie says. "Why even have a surveillance system?"

We watch it a second time, studying the background, but there is nothing to see.

The final footage and the best quality is from a gas station in Panama City where Randa stopped to fill up her car.

The footage is from a surveillance camera set up beneath the well-lit awning, but because of its position and the positioning of Randa's vehicle, only the back of her green Accord is visible.

Randa can be seen loosening her gas cap, swiping her credit card, removing the nozzle, inserting it into her car, and pumping gas for a few moments.

It's difficult to make out much detail, but she doesn't seem particularly distressed or upset. Actually, she appears to be daydreaming as she stands there waiting for the nozzle to click off.

No one else is around. No other cars pull up or take off. Nothing.

"Damnit," Reggie says. "Was hoping we'd see something since this is so close to where she went missing. And we could actually see something on this footage if there was something to see."

After pumping her gas, returning the nozzle, and replacing the cap, Randa closes the small gas cover and walks toward the store.

I follow her until she reaches the top edge of the frame and disappears. Nothing out of the ordinary. Nothing suspicious. Just a young woman walking. And then it goes black.

"Wait," Reggie says. "Go back. Just a few frames. Son of a bitch."

"What is it?"

"Were you watching her?" she asks.

"Yeah."

"I did too the first time, so this time I watched her car. Rewind it and watch only the car."

I do.

And there in the last few frames right before the footage ends and the screen goes blank, the front edge of a pair of solid black Pumas with Velcro flaps can be seen approaching the car.

Chapter Thirty-one

I try unsuccessfully for the next two days to find Josh Douglas.

After not showing up for his next class after we spoke, he emailed the chair of his department and told him for family reasons he had to take an emergency sabbatical effective immediately.

His home is empty.

He nor his wife are responding to calls, texts, or emails, and none of their friends or family seem to know where they are.

I talk to Sage Isaacson again, as well as several other students who attended the protest. They all say the same thing. No, Josh didn't show. Yes, he often wore black Pumas with Velcro flaps.

"You think it was him?" Anna says. "He was following her? He . . ."

"It's looking like a good possibility."

We're driving down to Sam and Daniel's to have dinner and give Merrill a little break. We're on Overstreet, the highway that connects Wewahitchka with Mexico Beach. It's late afternoon and the setting sun is burnishing the tips of the pines along the horizon in front of us.

"Think you'll find him?"

I nod. "Someone will. Lot of people looking for him. Disappearing is a lot harder than people think. Especially with a family."

"He could've killed them and left them behind."

"Could have, but we've checked the house. I bet they're just hiding somewhere."

She nods. "You ready to listen?"

"Sure."

"This is the episode about the other victim I was telling you about. It's all over the internet. Usually comes up when you do a search for *Randa Raffield*.

I nod and she starts the podcast.

"Welcome to another edition of *In Search of Randa Raffield*," Merrick says. "Today we have a very special episode for you. We're going to be talking about Annie Kathryn Harrison."

"A lot of people connect the disappearances of Annie Kathryn Harrison and Randa Raffield," Daniel says.

"Annie went missing about a month before Randa," Nancy says. "About fifty miles from where Randa did near Carabelle, Florida, on the same highway as Randa, and like Randa, only her car was found—locked. There's been no sign of her since."

"At first it seems a no-brainer to connect them," Merrick says. "And it makes you immediately think we're dealing with a serial killer. And it's possible, but . . ."

"But," Nancy says, "there are a lot of differences in the two cases too."

"For one," Daniel says, "though both young women were around the same age . . . Annie was a senior in high school. She lived in Carabelle, so, unlike Randa, she was close to home when it happened."

"In fact," Merrick says, "she was driving home from her after-school job, so also unlike Randa, she was basically in her own small town."

"Right," Daniel says. "But her car was found abandoned on the side of the road near the old light house. And like Randa her keys and wallet were gone and the car was locked, like she'd left on her own and intended to come back. But she never did."

"No, neither of them ever did," Merrick says. "But there's another big difference between Randa and Annie—one that Nancy really wants to talk about—and that is . . . unlike Randa, Annie was black."

"Yes, she was," Nancy says, "which is why her case hasn't gotten nearly the attention that Randa's has."

"I think there are other reasons too," Merrick says, "and we'll get into those, but let's talk about that for a minute."

"There's a phenomenon that's been described as Missing White Woman Syndrome—a phrase said to have been coined by Gwen Ifill of PBS—where certain victims get a disproportionate amount of media attention and coverage. It's true of white women like Randa Raffield. Even truer of white girls, especially white girls with blond hair and blue eyes like JonBenét

Ramsey. Think about the media frenzy when it comes to white female victims."

"It's undeniable," Daniel says.

"It's related to a concept a criminologist in the 1980s came up with called 'the ideal victim.' Nils Christie said that the ideal victim is the person who when hit by a crime is most readily given the complete and legitimate status of being a victim."

I think about how true this is and how I first encountered this in the Atlanta Child Murders where the victims were mostly poor black boys.

"We see this all the time in rape cases," Nancy says. "A sex worker is not afforded the victim status a young virgin is. It's the same with murder and the coverage of murder. Our culture and the coverage of our culture is racist and bigoted. A white girl like JonBenét or a white young woman like Randa Raffield will always get more coverage, more sympathy, more attention, better ratings than a victim like Annie Kathryn Harrison or any number of other victims—who by any objective measurement are no less victims."

"I couldn't agree more," Daniel says.

"I agree too," Merrick says, "but . . . in the two particular cases we're talking about today there are also other factors."

"Such as?" Nancy says.

"Well, part of what is so fascinating about the Randa Raffield case is not just that it is an unsolved murder, but it's an inexplicable mystery. There are so many unknowns, so many unanswered questions, so many possibilities leading to so many theories—any number of which could be right. Or none of them. Real mystery is a part of Randa's case in a way that it's not in Annie's. There are real, legitimate suspects in Annie's case. There just aren't so far in Randa's. There's a huge difference between not being able to make a case against someone you're pretty sure is the killer or killers versus not really having a single viable suspect. Annie Kathryn Harrison's brother was a drug dealer. Annie wasn't the only member of her family to be killed. Her brother was too. The tragedy of Annie's death is though she had helped her brother deal before, she had stopped and was really working hard to get her life on track. She was even working a shitty after-school job that paid very little—and it was coming home from that job that she got taken. And she got taken because her brother owed the wrong people too much money. He was warned. He ignored the warning. His sister was taken and executed. Not too long afterward, because I guess he still didn't heed the warning, he was gunned down in his front yard."

"Even if everything you're saying is true," Nancy says, "why doesn't Annie get as much attention as Randa and others? Especially when, as you say, she was doing so well and really working hard to have a better life. She was a child. An innocent. A victim. Every bit the complete and legitimate victim Randa is."

"I completely agree," Daniel says.

"I do too," Merrick says.

"And just because it's likely that Annie was taken by big-time drug suppliers or something to do with her brother's drug business, doesn't mean that she was. It's possible that she was taken by the same man who took Randa. I think it'd be foolish to rule it out."

"Then we won't," Daniel says.

When we get home later that night, there's another email waiting for me.

Clearly you do not listen, Mister John Jordan. Do you? I am not writing this for me. I am writing it for you. I sincerely do not want to hurt anyone you love. But I have warned you. I have given you a chance to let dead girls lie and you just won't do it, will you? Why? Is it because you have always won before? Have you ever lost? Have you ever not solved a case? You will not solve this one. You will not find Randa's remains. You will not catch me. I promise you that. All you will do is lose. And lose someone close to you. It is out of my hands now. I am not going to feel bad about having to do it. You are making me. You had your chance. What happens next is on you.

I forward it to Chris and to Reggie, but don't do anything else with it—except study it and reflect on it and try to understand its writer who doesn't use contractions, seems sincere about wanting me to heed his warning, and is absolutely convinced he will not get caught.

Chapter Thirty-two

"To me it comes down to Occam's razor," Cal Beckner is saying. "The most likely explanation is usually the right one. The simplest solution is most often the right one. Think about how many theories there are—how outlandish many of them are."

Cal Beckner has been on the show before. He's the private detective hired by the family to work on the case.

"And there are some truly outlandish ones out there," Nancy says.

"We should remind everyone that we don't give any airtime to those," Daniel says. "We're aware of them—the crazy theories flying around out there—but we don't get into them on our show."

"So what is Occam's razor?" Merrick asks. "And how does it apply to Randa's case?"

"It says something like out of competing theories, the one with the fewest assumptions should be selected."

"And in this case," Daniel says, "which theory is the one with the fewest assumptions?"

"I've gone back and forth on this one," Cal says. "Because I think there are two that are about tied. Either she committed suicide or someone killed her."

"And to some of our listeners who have only heard these two theories, I'm sure they're saying 'of course it's one of those two things, what else could it be?' So before Cal goes on, let me just mention a few of those other theories. Some say, though there is no evidence for this at all, that Randa was traveling with someone in a second vehicle, that she staged her disappearance, got in the car with them, and they went to Mexico together and are living the good life down there, that this whole thing was an ingenious plan to leave her life and start over."

"Which would mean she had an accomplice," Merrick says, "someone very close to her that was willing to do this—but no one close to her disappeared. And no one has ever said anything and you just don't keep a secret like that for twelve years."

"I also don't see her doing this to her parents," Daniel says, "leaving them to suffer like this if she was alive and could contact them to let them know she's okay."

"It's out there as a theory, but it's not even close to the most outrageous or outlandish," Merrick says. "There are groups of people who truly believe that Randa spontaneously combusted as she stood there on the side of the road that night, even point to some scorch marks on the ground. Say it's the only thing that would explain why her body was never found."

"And we're not going to get into the other theories of UFO abduction, Bigfoot, or that she discovered Atlantis while swimming in the bay," Nancy says. "The point is people are crazy and crazy theories are a distraction and we're serious about solving this case, about finding Randa and giving her family some sort of peace and justice."

"Right," Daniel says.

"Which is why Occam's razor should be employed," Cal says. "Among competing hypotheses, the one with the fewest assumptions should be chosen."

"Another way to say it," Daniel says, "is other things being equal, simpler explanations are generally better than more complex ones."

"But which one is it?" Nancy asks.

"That's the question, isn't it?" Cal says.

"It is," Merrick says, "and we were hoping you had the answer."

"That's the thing about this case," Cal says. "The moment you think you have an answer, what you really have is another question. Let's take the two most likely possibilities and the main question or assumption that accompanies them."

"Okay," Nancy says, "the first would be that Randa killed herself, that she was there to do harm to herself, that she had the hose and duct tape and books dealing with suicide in her car. So what's the question?"

"Where's the body?" Cal says. "If she killed herself somewhere around there—in the bay or the swamp—we should have found a body."

"True," Merrick says. "Now, the other most likely theory . . . A killer came along and killed her somewhere around there or abducted her and killed her somewhere else."

"With that one you also have the question of where is the body," Cal says. "No matter where he did it, you'd think her remains would have been discovered by now. Or that the killer would've been caught for another murder or crime—or that he wouldn't be able to keep it quiet for so long. He'd have to tell someone. Most of them do. But beyond all that . . . here is the real assumption that goes with this one. Is it really possible that a killer just happened upon the scene in the middle of nowhere at just the right moment? What are the chances?"

"It could happen," Nancy says.

"Absolutely it could," Cal says, "but is it more or less likely than her killing herself and us not finding the body?"

"Good question," Merrick says.

"I go back and forth between these two all the time," Daniel says. "And I can't figure out which one Occam's razor would make the most likely hypothesis. They each seem just as likely and unlikely."

"Yes they do," Cal says. "But today . . . I'm going with suicide. I know it's not as interesting or sexy as a serial killer, but . . . I believe the preponderance of evidence shows that Randa was suicidal, that that's what she was on her way to do—where we don't know—but that when she wrecked she went ahead and did it."

"But," Nancy says, "that leads to another glaring question. Her car was fine. If she was really headed to kill herself somewhere, why not just get back in her car and go do it? Why even get out of her car in the first place?"

Chapter Thirty-three

"Randa did *not* kill herself," Brenda Young is saying. "I don't know what the hell happened to her, but I know that. She wasn't the type. No question."

Brenda Young is a thick, nicely proportioned early thirties young woman with white-blond hair, pale skin, brown eyes beneath dark purple eyeshadow, and lots of colorful tattoos. She's wearing a loose black cotton dress, the fabric of which seems to be straining across her enormous breasts, and black boots that look to have been worn by the Wicked Witch of the West in the *Wizard of Oz*.

We are walking through the garden behind her juice bar, gift shop, and garden center in Tallahassee, where she has created a center for organic foods and locally produced artisan products for, according to her, hipsters and hippies.

Some eleven years ago, Brenda lived on the same floor as Randa in the UWF dorm and dated Chelsea Sylvester, the young woman who died shortly before Randa disappeared.

"Is her death or disappearance related to what happened to Chelsea?" I ask.

She frowns and her eyes glisten and in a moment, she nods. "I'm . . . I don't know how . . . directly, but . . . it has to be related."

"Can you tell me how?"

She nods. "Let's sit down over here."

She leads me to a cement bench at the back of the garden that looks like something from a cemetery.

We are facing the garden and the back of the old wooden building beyond it. The garden is verdant, the store vibrant, its front and back double doors open, allowing the bearded young boys in skinny jeans and dress shoes and the fat bearded old men in tie-dye shirts and overalls to flow freely in and out and through the property.

"It's been so long]now, you wouldn't think it would still upset me, but . . ."

"I understand," I say. "Take your time."

"There was something about Randa," she says. "A certain attraction. An attraction certain types of people were powerless over. Honestly, I'm not sure how aware of it she was. Some, I'd say. She definitely used it sometimes, but I think a lot of the time she didn't even realize it was happening—it was on, this tractor beam that issued forth from her goddessness."

"Were you drawn to her?"

She nods. "Some, sure, but . . . not in the way I'm talking about. Not like Chelsea was."

The trees around us are filled with wind chimes, which, when the breeze blows, joins with the waving of the limbs and branches to create a soft, hypnotic sound. Natural. Rhythmic. Transcendent.

"You and Chelsea were together, right?"

She nods. "Until Randa."

"They . . ."

"Chelsea was one of those drawn to her like a star caught in her gravitational pull. Completely powerless to do anything about it."

"Were they lovers? A couple? Did you and Chelsea break up?"

"They were . . . whatever people were with Randa. I don't know what you'd call it. Just . . . drawn in. Chelsea was obsessed with her. She didn't break up with me. Didn't have to. I just sort of ceased to exist. Or . . . orbited out of her . . . I don't know. Our relationship ended. But I still was in her life because . . . I knew it wouldn't be long until Randa was on to the next object she sucked in, and Chelsea would be devastated."

"And that happened?"

"Sooner than I predicted," she says.

"Were you angry at Randa?"

"Sure, but more just concerned for Chelsea. And I was right to be. I predicted she'd be devastated, but I had no idea just how decimated she would be. She started drinking and taking drugs like someone serious about doing real harm to themselves. I tried to help her, to save her. She only wanted Randa. Randa, who did have a huge heart, came to see her, tried to talk to her, but . . . Chelsea told her if she couldn't be with her she didn't want to live. Now I don't know if Chelsea really meant to kill herself or just accidentally overdosed, but either way . . . Randa felt responsible, which is why she . . . acted the way she did, took off like she did. It's what put her in the situation she was in when whatever happened to her did."

"So you don't think she was suicidal?"

"I know she wasn't. We talked about it. She had no intention of harming herself, but . . . she was really upset, like . . . she went a little nuts. So she put herself in whatever peril she found herself in."

"What about the items found in her car that indicate she was suicidal or thinking about committing suicide?"

She turns and looks at me with genuine surprise and not a little disgust.

"You're the detective heading up the investigation?" she asks.

I nod.

"How can you be so . . . uninformed?"

"Good question," I say. "One I ask all the time."

"I'm serious."

"I am too, actually."

"Randa worked at the suicide hotline on campus. She helped a shit ton of people. Some of the people she helped, especially the young women, would often give her things—the things that were feeding their suicidal thoughts or the very things they had intended to use to harm themselves. You can't imagine the pills and blades and shit she was given. Whatever was in her car was there because someone grateful for her help gave it to her. How can you solve her case if you don't know that?"

"I can't," I say, "which is why now I do. Thank you."

"Sorry. I just . . . that was uncalled for. I shouldn't take shit out on you. My bad. I didn't get to meditate this morning and I can tell. I'm a mess. Please forgive me."

"Did you ever confront Randa?" I ask. "Did you let her know you blamed her for Chelsea's death?"

"We talked. I could tell she felt bad. I . . . I only blamed her for getting involved with Chelsea to begin with. If she had just shown some self-restraint . . . none of this would have happened. But she had none."

"Are you saying if she hadn't gotten involved with Chelsea, not only would Chelsea still be alive, but Randa would too?"

She nods, and I wonder if it's because she killed her.

"When was the last time you saw Randa?"

"The day she died," she says.

Interesting she said *died* instead of *disappeared*. So definitive. Does she know what happened to Randa? Is she subconsciously saying she does?

"Where?"

"Hallway in the dorm."

"What'd she say? How'd she act?"

"We didn't speak, but she acted fine. Like her same old self. Like she had gotten over what had happened to Chelsea."

"How'd that make you feel?" I ask.

"Not great, but . . . I was feeling bad anyway. Chelsea had not come out to her parents. They didn't know anything about me. Treated me like shit at the funeral. I was . . . I had had enough that day, I can tell you that."

"What'd you do about it?"

"Turned within. It was around that time I started meditating and using aromatherapy and getting in touch with my inner goddess."

"We were going through Randa's things and found a pair of shoes that weren't hers," I say. "Do you know if her boyfriend—"

"Which one?"

"Josh. Do you know if Josh had a pair of black Pumas with flaps on top?"

She nods. "He did. I know he did because . . . I had some too. It's the only thing we ever talked about. Literally. The only thing."

Chapter Thirty-four

"You okay?" I ask Jerry Raffield when he opens his front door.

He frowns and shrugs, then eventually nods, but I can tell he's not. All the color has drained from his face and his pale skin is clammy.

Seeing him reminds me that I still need to follow up on the lead he gave me the last time I was here—Bill Lee, Randa's alleged molester—and I decide that Scarlett George, Randa's aunt and Bill's girlfriend, will probably be the best way to do it. Besides, I need to talk to her anyway.

"This is Chris," I say as we walk into the study of his Seaside home. "He's gonna help us track the person who sent it."

The two men exchange greetings and Chris rushes over to the computer and begins to click and bang around on the keyboard.

We are here because earlier in the evening Jerry received an email from his daughter—well, someone claiming to be his daughter.

From: Randa Raffield
Sent: Tuesday, October 4, 2016, 5:37 PM
    To: Jerry Raffield
    Subject: Leave Me Alone
    Message: What if I don't want to be found?

MICHAEL LISTER

Not only was the message emailed to Jerry, but it was posted on a few different Randa Raffield missing persons forums.

Jerry's phone vibrates and he pulls it out of his pocket.

"I keep getting calls and emails and messages," he says. "Everybody is freaking out over this. I . . . I'm just not sure what to say. Hell, I don't know what to think."

I nod. "Sorry this is happening."

"It's . . . all this new activity on the case has it . . . all stirred up again. It's like it just happened."

"I know. I'm sorry. I just hope it's worth it. I hope it means we're getting closer to finding the truth."

"It's not the same sender emailing you," Chris says.

"It's not?" I say. "You sure?"

"Nowhere near the level of technical sophistication," he says. "I think we just might be able to trace this one." He looks at Jerry. "Mind if I take your computer?"

"What if she emails me again?" he says.

Chris frowns, then looks heartbroken for the sad, daughterless dad. "If that happens, I'll let you know the moment it does. I'll take good care of . . . everything . . . and . . . find whoever sent this."

That night, after just a few minutes of sleep, I wake startled, heart pounding, my head sweating.

Easing out of bed, trying not to wake Anna, I walk through the dim house to the back patio and sit on one of the old, unpainted wooden chairs.

Beyond the craggy cypress trees at its edge, a three-quarters moon looms above Lake Julia, its reflection floating on the dark, shimmering surface below.

My mind is racing, thoughts and questions about Randa flying at me too quick to contemplate or answer.

I attempt to use my breathing to slow my heart and mind, but my efforts are mostly ineffectual.

"You okay?" Anna asks.

I turn to see her standing at the partially open French doors.

I nod.

"What is it?"

"Woke up startled."

She steps down onto the cement pad and over to me, sitting on the arm of the chair as she puts her arms around me.

"You should've woke me up."

"You're not getting enough sleep as it is," I say.

"Doesn't matter. Is it the case?"

I nod again. "I've got no traction, just spinning, flailing about. Not getting anywhere. Not sure I will."

Her touch is tender, her caress calming.

"You've been here before," she says. "Many times."

"This one seems different. I'm not sure I can close it."

"My money's on you," she says, "but what if you can't? You have other unsolved cases."

"Not like this. I just can't get my bearings, there's nothing to grab on to. I'm down the rabbit hole and I just keep falling."

"Why?" she asks. "What's different about this case?"

"Too many unknowns, too much information, too many suspects, too many possibilities," I say.

"Is it the emails, the taunting?"

"It's all of it. The picture sent to Daniel, the email sent to Jerry."

"But what about the one sent to you?" she says. "Are you worried about us? Are you . . . Is it what's upsetting you the most?"

I shake my head.

"I've seen you find peace before," she says. "Even in the midst of uncertainty and loss. You can do it again—even if you don't solve it, even if you have to live with not knowing what really happened to Randa and who's behind it. What do you have to do to get to that point?"

I shake my head again. "Not ready to go there yet. Not ready to give up, to . . . let go."

"Fine, but you've got to be able to function, to sleep, to have some sort of peace so your mind can . . . do what it does."

"You're helping with that," I say. "So is the moon and the lake."

She tries unsuccessfully to stifle a yawn.

"Thank you," I say. "I'm okay. Go back to bed. I'll be back in there beside you in just a few."

"You sure?"

"Yes. Taylor will be up before you know it. And I'll be in there beside you before you know it."

But I wasn't. Instead I went for a drive. I returned to the scene of the crime, the place where Randa Raffield vanished from the face of the earth.

Chapter Thirty-five

Overstreet is dark and damp, and a moist fog hovers just above the road.

It's difficult to see and I'm driving far faster than is safe.

The way I feel, I want to drive even faster, but images of Anna and the girls arrive unbidden and I back off the accelerator.

I tell myself I'm just driving, that I have no agenda, no destination, but I know when I'm being lied to, know where I'll wind up and why I'll be there.

It's the gravitational pull Brenda Young spoke about. I'm being drawn to the mystery, attracted to the place where in one way it all began and in another it all ended.

Images from the investigation float toward me like oncoming headlights, bits of information, insights, and impossibilities.

Lost in thought about the case and operating on autopilot, I lose time, and only come out of the state I'm in as I park in the exact spot Randa had.

I get out.

It's late, the highway empty.

I check my phone. I'm on the edge of the continent. Service is spotty here. At the moment I have none. I have to figure that it was far worse at the beginning of 2005. Could Randa have even used her phone if she wanted to?

I walk in the direction the dogs traced her scent, stumbling in the darkness along the uneven shoulder of the road.

To my left, the nocturnal noises of the swamp are soft and muted. To my right, beyond the breeze, a hint of the incessant tide rolling in and rolling out. Rolling in and rolling out.

I have to walk around the small popup tent being used as the water and coordination station for the search of the swamp behind it.

On the other side, I nearly trip over the pile of pictures, flowers, candles, cards, balloons, posters, and ribbons that constitute the Randa Raffield shrine. The candles are unlit, long since extinguished by the breeze blowing in off the bay and rain from earlier in the evening.

I pause for a moment and look down at the expressions of love and concern, hope and solidarity. White teddy bears with big red hearts. Swim caps and goggles. UWF attire. Notes. Signs. Drawings.

We Love You Randa. Come Home Soon. RIP Randa Raffield. Thoughts and Prayers. We will find your killer. I am Randa Raffield and so are You!

I continue walking, somehow more melancholy now, an even greater heaviness resting upon me.

Each step labored, each stumble nearly a fall.

Eventually, I reach the spot where the dogs stopped because her scent ended, and pause to look around.

"RANDA," I yell into the dark void of empty night. "RANDA. WHERE'D YOU GO? WHAT REALLY HAPPENED? WHO TOOK YOU? WHAT DID HE DO TO YOU?"

The clouds above me part, letting marginally more moonlight through, but no answers or insight of illumination pierces the dark veil of my benightedness.

What are you doing here? You should be at home in bed beside your beautiful wife. What's wrong with you? Who's this helping? What good is it doing? Is this more useful than sleep and the perchance to dream a solution, an insight, an answer?

Ignoring the questions, I cross the street, walk a short ways, and enter Windmark.

A few lights dot the darkness but it remains mostly a ghost town.

A whistling wind whines through the empty buildings and through the trees.

I continue farther into what looks like a small, abandoned seaside town.

Beneath the pale, diffuse moonlight, the deserted development is eerie and unsettling, and only adds to my disorientation and disquietude.

There in the distance, I see Randa, her auburn hair flowing in the bay breeze, its tips streaked with moonlight, her green eyes glowing, her pale skin translucent.

I blink and she is gone.

And though I know what I've just witnessed is a figment, a fiction, a fragment of memory and imagination, I still find it unsettling—and a troubling sign of my altered state.

A noise coming up behind me startles me out of my dissociative state and I whip around, bringing up my weapon and pointing it at the tall figure in the dark.

"Steady there, mate," the man says. "I'm just walking my dog, aren't I?"

He's old, tall, and lean, with longish, fine white-blond hair and a much and deeply lined face. His hands are up. A leash extends from his right one to a large dog on the ground below.

"Sorry," I say, holstering my firearm.

"Mate, are you okay?"

I nod.

"You want me to telly a . . . ambulance for you?"

I shake my head. "I'm okay. Sorry I startled you."

"Think I'm the one what startled you. You sure you're okay? Want some tea and a biscuit or something? Get you right as rain. Drink a little tea, have a little biscuit, and Bob's your uncle you'll be fit again in two shakes of a lamb's tail."

"You British Bob?" I ask.

"I sometimes answer to that name. How the hell'd you know that?"

"I'm John Jordan with the Gulf County Sheriff's Department," I say. "Left a card on your door. Been trying to reach you."

"Oh, right, well, I've been meaning to ring you, but been . . ."

"Busy walking your dog?"

He smiles. "Among other things. Intended to call you though, I swear it, mate."

"Did your neighbor tell you what I wanted to talk to you about?"

He nods.

"Is that why you were hesitant to return my calls?"

"Really have been busy, but . . . that's a bad business, ain't it, and I must admit I weren't too keen on gettin' involved."

"Why exactly?"

"No offense to you, I'm sure, but . . . I ain't had the best of experiences with coppers in my past, I can tell you that."

"Were you here the night Randa Raffield went missing?"

He shakes his head. "Came in the next day. Had nowhere to stay back then. We was just beginning construction, wasn't we?"

"Anyone or anything suspicious or out of the ordinary when you arrived?"

He frowns and shakes his head. "Bloody hell, man," he says. "I . . . I . . . This is why I . . . didn't want to . . . It didn't even occur to me to be suspicious of it until recently, did it? I swear, mate. But . . . they were late pouring my foundation because they had to fix and re-level the dirt beneath it where it had been disturbed the night before. They had to adjust the rebar and grade pins. It's probably nothing, most likely an animal, but . . . there it is. I was going to tell you, wasn't I? I just . . . But . . . you can't tear down a one-point-six-million-dollar home because something might be buried beneath it."

Chapter Thirty-six

"We can't just dig under a man's house because some dirt was disturbed before he poured his foundation," Reggie is saying.

"But—"

"Not any house, but especially a million-dollar Windmark mansion."

"It's not just a little disturbed dirt," I say. "It was enough to make him question whether or not she could be under there. And it happened the night she went missing—just a few hundred yards from where her car was found."

"It's probably more like a mile, but . . . I understand what you're saying. I do."

"I did some research," I say. "There are non-destructive ways to at least see if she's buried there. We could use a ground-penetrating radar to—"

"If and when we decide to do it, we can get FDLE to do it."

"*If?*" I say, my voice rising. "*If?*"

"Yes, if. We have to tread very carefully—and not just from a—"

"Tread carefully? This could be—"

"John, no judge is going to give us a warrant with what we've got. We've got nothing. Some innuendo and disturbed dirt. That's it."

"What if I can get the homeowner to sign a Permission to Search?"

"That might be a direction we can go at some point, but . . . do you know how many Permission to Searches get suppressed at trial? All the homeowner has to claim is that he signed it under duress, that you forced him, threatened him, and it could get tossed—along with anything we might find."

"But, listen to me . . . if I'm—"

"You okay, John? You sleeping?"

"Not lately, no. Why? I'm okay."

"You seem a little strung out," she says. "Is this case getting to you?"

I hesitate a moment, sigh, and nod. "Yeah. They all do. But this one more than most. I'm fine. Just didn't sleep last night."

"You've got to take care of yourself," she says. "You won't be any good for anybody—including Randa—if you come apart at the seams. Now, listen to me. Get some rest. Take care of yourself. I'm not saying *no* to going the Permission to Search route, but a court order would be far better, a search warrant when we have probable cause. So let's work on getting that. Okay? Find me that. Then we'll do the sonar scans. Let's exhaust every other possibility. Okay? See if we can find probable cause. If not, we'll revisit the Permission to Search. Seem reasonable?"

I nod.

"So get some rest. Get yourself together. Once you're not exhausted, exhaust all the other possibilities, and if you still haven't found her, we'll look under British Bob's McMansion."

"Okay."

"And if you find her without us having to look under his foundation, I don't tell anybody you wanted us to."

I smile. "Thanks."

"Now—"

She stops as both our phones begin to vibrate—an occurrence that never brings good news.

Merrick is calling her and Chris is calling me—both about the same thing.

A man claiming to be Randa's killer has just posted a video online.

"Take a look at it," Chris says, "while I work on tracking down where it came from."

After we disconnect our calls, Reggie opens her laptop on her desk and I walk around to her, and we watch the video together.

The In Search of Randa Raffield website has been hacked. All that is on it now is an image of her abandoned car on the side of the road, beneath it the words *I confess*.

Clicking on the image takes us to a site called IKilledRandaRaffield.com. On it, an average-size man is sitting in a dark room. He's wearing a black hoodie and his face has been blacked out and his voice digitally distorted.

"Who I am is not important," he says, his altered voice deep and demented. "What I did is. I am a man with a demon inside me. I'm a slave to his desires. I wish I could control him better, but I can't. I'm sorry, but I can no more control him than you can the tide. Be clear about this. I'm not asking for forgiveness. I neither want it or deserve it. I only want to bring closure to Randa's family. Mr. and Mrs. Raffield, I am sorry for killing your daughter. I truly am. Please know it was quick. She didn't suffer. In a way, her death was like a baptism into her new life. I drowned her in the bay and gave her body back to the sea, from whence all life proceeded. I had no idea her body wouldn't be discovered or that that fact would lead to so much fanciful speculation. For that too I am sorry. And I'm sorry for not contacting you sooner. I should have. Just know Randa is at peace and I hope now you can be too."

Without saying a word, Reggie clicks for the video to replay.

The room the man is in is so dark nothing is clearly visible—part of a dark curtain, his hoodie. A dark figure in front of a darker background. That is it.

"Think it's real?" she asks.

I shrug.

"Gut?" she says.

I shake my head. "But that's all it is. Just an instinct."

"Mine says the same thing. Either way, I hope Chris can—"

My phone starts vibrating again. It's Chris.

"It's the same person who sent the email to the dad—Randa's dad. Same guy. And I've got a location on him."

Chapter Thirty-seven

"*F uck*," Chris says.

"What?" I say. "What is it?"

"Spoke too soon. Don't have them. Thought I did. Sorry. I'll keep working on it. Think I'm close."

I want to throw my phone across the room, but find the strength to refrain.

"Okay," I say. "Just keep at it. Let me know when you have something."

"Hopefully it won't be long."

"Anything stand out to you about the video?" I ask. "Or how it was posted or—"

"Just that there are two of them," he says.

"Whatta you mean?"

"Huh? Two people. To make the video. It's very subtle but . . . at the very end . . . there's the slightest . . . the camera moves. Someone is holding it."

"I watched it twice and missed that," I say.

When I'm off the call, Reggie and I watch the video again.

"There it is," she says when the camera moves right before the video ends. "How'd we miss that? Well, I know how you did. You need some sleep. But how did I miss that?"

"I should've seen it," I say.

"Go home and get some sleep," she says. "That's an order."

"But—"

"It's an order. Don't so much as think about the case. Think about other things. Turn your phone off and sleep. Sleep a long time, then call me when you get up."

I try to do as I'm told—with the exception of turning off my phone—but as tired as I am, when I lie down I am unable to fall asleep.

The house is empty and quiet.

Dad had a doctor's appointment and Anna and Taylor went with him and Verna.

The shades are drawn, the curtains closed. The room is dark. The fan is on. All the conditions are right, but I can't fall asleep.

When I close my eyes I see Randa. In vivid detail—her young, muscular swimmer's body, her silky, auburn-tinted hair. Her huge, sparkling green eyes and the complexity of the person behind them they reveal.

I toss and turn, roll onto my right side, then my back, then my left. I pull Anna's pillow to me and hold it the way I hold her when we spoon to fall asleep. Nothing works.

Sleep eludes me.

Eventually I give up, grab my phone, and turn the *In Search of Randa Raffield* podcast back on.

"As we've mentioned before," Daniel is saying, "Merrick is working on a book about this case. He's a former reporter and a very good writer and we know it's going to be a good book you'll want to read when it comes out. But that means that Merrick is under deadline so he can't be with us today. Nancy is here. Say *hi* Nancy."

"Hi Nancy," she says.

"And we're joined by a special guest today," Daniel adds. "Roger Lamott. You'll remember Roger is the only witness. He saw Randa after her accident and called the police. Welcome, Roger."

"Thanks."

"Thanks for being on the show," Nancy says. "We really appreciate it."

"No problem."

I press Pause and call Daniel.

"Are y'all doing a show right now?" I ask.

"No. Why? What's up? Everything okay. You sound—"

"When'd you do the show with Roger Lamott?"

"Week, week and a half ago. Why?"

"How'd you get him?"

"Merrick did. Took a while. Just kept trying. Finally he agreed to do it. Why?"

"I've been trying to talk to him. Feel like he's been avoiding me. Won't answer my calls. Won't return my messages."

"Oh, shit, wish we'd've known. We would've let you know."

"Did he come and record with y'all in person or call in?"

"Called in. I've never seen the guy. He was awkward to interview. Weird. Acted like he didn't want to be doing it. Had to pull every word out of him. I don't know. Have you listened to the interview?"

"Not yet. Why?"

"He came on the show to clear his name. He's very hostile to local law enforcement. I think that's the real reason Merrick wasn't on the show. Think he thought he'd have to say something to defend Reggie and . . . Anyway, Lamott said he's lived under a cloud of suspicion for twelve years now because of leaks, lies, and innuendos from investigators."

"Even if that's true, and I really don't think it is, there's a new sheriff and a new investigation—all new investigators."

"I pointed that out, but . . . I don't know. Didn't seem to do any good. Want me to call him, see if he'll answer for me, see if I can get him to meet with you? I think we had a pretty good rapport by the time the show ended."

"Would you? I'd really appreciate that. Thanks."

After ending the call I start the podcast again, but am distracted by thoughts of Roger Lamott and his motive for avoiding me and saying what he did on the show.

I pause the podcast.

Had Lamott had a bad experience with one of the previous sheriffs? Was there talk around town about him being the killer? Or was he going on the offensive as a way of disguising his defensiveness?

I decide I can ask him myself when my phone starts vibrating a moment later and I see that it's him.

Chapter Thirty-eight

"Hear you're lookin' for me," he says.

"You heard right."

"I ain't avoiding you or nothin'," he says. "I just ain't got nothin' to say. Nothin' to add. All I did was see her on the highway, stop and ask if she needed help, and call the cops as I pulled away. That's it. And for that, for happening to be on that road at that time and for trying to do the right thing . . . I get suspected for the rest of my damn life. It ain't right. And I'm sick of it."

"I genuinely don't know of anyone saying you had anything to do with Randa's disappearance."

"Well, you're new and not listening I guess."

"The sheriff's new too. It's a new investigation. We're trying to get to the truth. That's all. Do you have something to hide?"

"The hell would you ask me that? See? I told you I was a suspect."

"You're acting suspicious. You're acting like you have something to hide. That's why I asked."

"You sound like everybody else," he says. "Guilty 'til proven innocent. Just like all the rest."

He ends the call without another word and when I call back it goes straight to voicemail.

I try a few more times and on my fourth attempt Chris Anderson beeps in.

"I've got him," he says. "This time for real. Same person that sent the email to the dad definitely uploaded the confession video online."

"Where?" I ask, jumping up from the bed and pulling on my clothes.

"You're not gonna believe this," he says. "Dalkeith."

Dalkeith is a small unincorporated area of farms and rural route old home places, dirt roads, dilapidated mobile homes, and river camps. It's located between Port St. Joe and Wewahitchka, but is a little closer to Wewa.

"Really?" I say.

"What if her killer has been right here, that close to us, all this time?"

"Great work. Thank you. Text me the address. I'm gonna call Reggie. Hang tight. As soon as we secure the scene I'll call you to come look at his computer."

I end the call with Chris and tap in Reggie's number.

"We got him," I say. "Chris tracked him down."

"Where?"

I tell her.

"Dalkeith?"

"I'm headed there now. Gonna call dispatch and have a deputy meet me there."

"Bad wreck in White City," she says. "Everybody on the north end of the county is tied up with that. I'll meet you."

"You sure?"

"Actually already headed that way. Just left the scene of the accident."

"Anyone hurt?"

"Yeah," she says, "but no fatalities. Log truck coming down off the bridge too fast. Hit two cars stopped in the road waiting for a dog to get out of the way. So . . . what do we have?"

"Chris says this is definitely the location of the guy who sent the email to Jerry Raffield and posted the confession video on the In Search of Randa Raffield website."

"But not the one who Snapchated the picture of Randa or who's been emailing you?"

"Right. Though I guess he could be using different accounts or IP addresses or something. Just don't know enough about it to even guess, but Chris says he thinks it's two different people."

"So this could be . . . May not be the killer. Wow. It's interesting. To me they all seem credible—the different emails, the Snapchat image, the confession. Hard to believe one of them might be a . . . fraud."

"Could be dealing with two killers," I say. "Work or worked together but now live in and communicate from two different places."

"In one way it would make more sense—in terms of them getting away with it, helping each other with every aspect of the abduction, murder, and hiding the body—but . . . in another . . . you'd think one of them would've talked by now."

"Oh whoever it is, is talking," I say.

"No doubt," she says. "Let's go see what else they have to say."

"Texting you the address," I say. "See you there."

"Wait for me," she says. "Don't go in without me."

Chapter Thirty-nine

The faded and falling-apart old trailer sits less than fifty yards back off the highway, fronted by a weed-infested yard filled with junk and trash.

We drive down the dirt and mud driveway, passing piles of aluminum cans, old appliances, abandoned toys, and two vehicles, their hoods up, their tires flat, trash stacked on their roofs and trunks.

Near the front door of the trailer, tethered to a metal rod in the ground by a chain, is a snarling, squat, bound-up brown and white pit bull.

Reggie and I had met at the little Dalkeith convenience store and gas station. She had parked her car there and is now riding with me.

"Can this really be the place?" she asks. "Property records have it listed to a single female with no record. Wonder if she has a boyfriend living with her?"

Most of the skirting around the bottom of the trailer is missing, revealing a collapsing floor support underneath, and faded, wet, pink insulation falling out of it like stuffing from a dying homemade sock monkey.

We park at the end of the dirt drive near one of the abandoned vehicles and get out.

Avoiding the trash and mud and angrily barking pit bull, we make our way to the door and knock on it.

"Hope that chain holds," Reggie says. "Hate to have to shoot a dog."

It takes a few minutes but eventually the warped aluminum door is opened a crack by a chubby, pasty white boy of about seventeen with black hair and bad skin who looks like he just woke up.

"Gulf County Sheriff's Department," Reggie says. "Who are you?"

"Huh?" he asks, rubbing sleep from his squinting eyes.

"What's your name?" I ask.

"Alec," he says. "Alec Henry. My mom's at work."

"What's her name? You alone here?"

"Yeah. Ah, June. June Stapleton. She'll be back . . . sometime this evening."

"Can we come in, Alec?" Reggie asks, pushing on the door and walking in without waiting for him to answer the question.

It's dim and quiet, the only illumination coming from the light over the stove in the kitchen, the only sound the hum of central AC.

The inside of the small, narrow house trailer is only slightly less cluttered with junk and trash as the outside. Of course, it could be more cluttered. It's just too difficult to tell in the dark.

Alec is wearing either chef pants or pajama bottoms—I can't tell which—with cats on them and a too-tight wife beater.

"What do you do, Alec?" Reggie asks.

"Workin' on my GED."

"How old are you?"

"Seventeen."

"Why aren't you in school?"

"Y'all truancy? I'm all legit. Old enough to drop out of that boring shit and still get my degree on my own."

"Who lives here with you and your mom?" I ask.

"Just us."

"Make a lot of mess for there just being two of you," Reggie says.

"Yeah, we been talkin' 'bout gettin' a maid."

He's serious. No hint of humor in what he's saying.

"Where's your computer?" I ask.

He hesitates a moment, then jerks his head back toward an old desktop at a makeshift desk in the corner of the crowded room.

It's old and out of date and covered with papers and magazines.

"No," I say. "Your computer."

"The one you uploaded the video with," Reggie says. "The one you used to send the email from Randa to her dad."

He tries to look confused but can't pull it off.

Suddenly he bolts toward the hallway.

I lunge at him, slamming into him and knocking him down, his body putting a hole in the thin, brittle paneling of the wall.

Putting my knee in his back and pulling his hands around behind him, I begin to cuff him.

Reggie withdraws her weapon and a small penlight and begins down the hallway.

"Anybody else here?" she asks.

He doesn't respond. Too busy expressing his discomfort and pain.

"Don't get somebody killed, Alec," she says. "Is anybody else here?"

He still doesn't answer her.

"Gulf County Sheriff's Department," she yells down the dark hallway. "Anybody here? Come out with your hands up. This is your last warning."

She feels along the wall and eventually finds a light switch, but nothing happens when she flips it.

I pull Alec to his feet, press him against the wall, and pat him down.

"Why were you running?" I ask. "Where's your computer? Who helped you record the confession? Is anyone else here?"

"What confession? I didn't confess to anything? Ain't done anything."

"Where's your mom work? Anyone else here?"

"Dollar Store."

"Which one?

"General."

"Is she there now?"

"Yeah. I told you."

Footsteps. Someone running.

I spin around.

Two loud shots from the hall.

Shoving Alec down face-first on the floor, I withdraw my weapon and start down the dark hall.

"Reggie," I yell. "Reggie. Are you okay?"

"Oh no. Oh . . . *Motherfucker*," Reggie yells. "*Goddamnit.*"

"What is it? You hit?"

"Quick. Call an ambulance," she says. "I just shot a kid."

Chapter Forty

"His little brother held the camera and helped him make the video," Chris is saying. "It's all here on his computer. All the outtakes and unaltered audio and video."

He and I are in the small evidence room of the sheriff's department, the laptop on the table in front of him, his gloved fingers dancing across the keyboard and track pad.

"Sent the email to Jerry too," he says. "Didn't really even try to hide anything. It's all in here. Not behind any security walls or anything."

"Anything in there indicate why he did it?"

"Because he could," he says. "Just thought it'd be cool. See how many views he could get. How's Reggie?"

I shrug. "Waiting to see her."

He shakes his head. "That's . . . so . . . I just can't . . ."

"I know. Anything else on his computer?"

"All kinds of shit."

"Anything else related to Randa? Did he send the image of her or the emails to me?"

He shakes his head again. "Wasn't him."

"Anything else? Other crimes or—"

"Definitely some cyberbullying and . . . theft . . . some . . . sexual stuff that . . . it looks like he made it and . . . it looks illegal. We know his brother's under-age . . . so . . ."

"Keep looking," I say. "Let me know what else you find. Be careful with everything. Back it up. Guard chain of custody. When you finish, we'll turn it over to the FDLE lab and see if they can come up with anything else."

Reggie appears as if she's aged over ten years in less than ten hours.

Her eyes are hollow and vacant, small and puffy, her normally dark skin pale and splotchy, stretched across her skull like a too-tight drumhead.

Her movements are slow—like her labored breathing and everything about her.

She seems to be doing everything from a great distance away, distracted, damaged, dissociative.

She's in shock—and acts like it.

"I've asked FDLE to investigate the incident," she says. "They probably would have anyway, but . . . I'm cooperating fully with them. And I want you to too."

She has yet to make eye contact with me. She's standing behind her desk, a pencil in her hand though she isn't writing and there is no paper in front of her.

"The . . . main . . . thing . . . I wanted to . . . say is . . . don't let any of . . . this . . . interfere with your investigation. Don't stop. Don't get . . . distracted by . . ."

"Forget about all that for now," I say. "Talk to me. Tell me what you're thinking, how you're doing."

She shakes her head and frowns. "Don't know what I could've done differently. He came flying out at me from the side with . . . something in his hand. I . . . I just . . . reacted. I . . . Why the fuck wasn't he in school?"

The kid, a large-for-his-age eleven-year-old, ran at Reggie from the bathroom with part of a broken and black-taped muffler in his hands.

"Exactly. Why wasn't he? Why was he helping his brother in criminal enterprises? Why didn't his brother tell him to come out, tell us he was there? It's all on them. Not you. You didn't do anything wrong."

"I . . . I should have found working lights. I should have waited for . . ."

"You did everything right in a difficult, unfolding situation," I say. "I should've been back there with you. I took too long with Alec. It's more my fault than yours—and it's not your fault at all."

"I keep playing it over and over in my head," she says. "Trying to remember exactly what happened, exactly what I was thinking, if I could've done anything differently. The thing is . . . I can't think of anything I could've done differently. And I know given the circumstances . . . I . . . I did okay. But . . . all that's just intellectual. In my heart I just keep saying I killed a kid."

"But you didn't," I say. "You only clipped him. He's gonna be okay. We're all just grateful you're not a better shot."

She almost smiles at that. Almost, but not quite.

"I know you feel like shit and you're in shock," I say. "It's understandable. Just go home and get some rest. Sleep for a while. Give yourself time to get over it. But as you do, give yourself a break. Don't keep going over and over it. Don't beat yourself up or blame yourself for the obvious criminal failings of others. We should've never had to be in that situation. That's on them. Not you."

"Other thing is . . ." she says. "This'll be shit I have to deal with. More fodder for my critics. More ammunition for my political opponents. It's embarrassing. And I'm sure there will be some sort of lawsuit against me from the family. It's just . . . the nightmare of all this . . . is just beginning."

"Don't borrow trouble from tomorrow," I say. "Today has enough of its own. We'll deal with everything as it comes and none of it will be as bad as it seems right now. Okay? For now, let it all go and just take care of yourself. Tell Merrick all about it and let him hold you and care for you. Get a big hug from Rain and your mom. Hug them back and remember all the good you're surrounded by. Then show back up here tomorrow and let's catch the evil bastard who got Randa. Okay?"

Chapter Forty-one

"Murder is not entertainment," Nancy is saying. "It's violent and depraved and as awful as anything humans have ever come up with. Criminal investigation is not entertainment. It's not just there for our enjoyment. We do this podcast and others like it because we're interested in murder and homicide investigation. We're fascinated by it. And we try to make an entertaining show, but . . . murder is not entertainment. What law enforcement does is not for our amusement. What the families of missing and murdered victims go through is unimaginable. It's a deep, brutal, bitter, acute pain that is merciless and relentless and that has no cure."

"Well said," Daniel says. "An important reminder we all need to hear. All of us who do this and listen to it."

I'm driving to Daniel and Sam's. Anna is already there waiting for me. She, Daniel, and I are driving over to East Point to have dinner at Nancy's place. Merrick and Reggie were meant to be going too, but I can't imagine they will after what she's been through today.

"If you've ever been touched by true crime," Nancy says, "I mean if brutality and violation and loss has touched you directly, then you'll know what I mean. It's not fun or funny. It's not amusing or entertaining. It's devastating. Painful beyond belief."

"We get that this is entertaining," Merrick says. "We do. And we're not saying there's anything wrong with that. And the last thing we're trying to do is alienate any of our listeners. But . . . we've seen enough and heard enough to know we needed to address this head-on."

"Nothing wrong with being entertained by what we and others are doing," Nancy says. "It becomes wrong when we look at it as purely entertainment, here for our pleasure and titillation, when we forget that these are real people who had unimaginably horrible things happen to them, whose families suffer every single day."

"Right," Daniel says. "If we lose empathy or compassion for the real people we're talking about— or if we do anything that leads our audience to do that, to stop caring and feeling . . . then we've failed."

"According to some of the emails and messages we get, we have," Nancy says. "We've done just that. Some of them are so callous and . . . well, cringeworthy."

"So we're just sending out a little reminder to everyone, saying check yourself as we check ourselves. Just to say take a moment, take a look, be aware, remember these are real people, hurting people we're talking about here."

"Tell you another thing that really bothers me," Daniel says. "And this is just me. I'm not saying it's wrong for everybody, but . . . while we're on the subject . . . I've heard some true crime podcasts that are essentially comedy routines throughout the entire show. And they don't just laugh at criminals and killers and cops, but they make fun of victims and their families too. Actually try to be funny at their expense."

"Yeah, I know you have a real problem with those," Merrick says, "but I don't. I thought they were using humor—sometimes very sick humor—to get some good points across."

"I'm with Daniel on this one," Nancy says. "Don't want any part of anything where nothing's sacred. Victims are sacred. Their families are sacred. And if we're talking about the same podcast . . . at least one of them got so many case facts wrong it was . . . that was even worse than the gallows humor. Their show was sloppy. So many errors. And not just because they were sacrificing nuance for humor, but just getting the underlying case facts wrong. It was unconscionable."

"Do you think . . ." Daniel begins. "I'm just thinking that . . . I wonder if those who are drawn to either create or listen to unsolved murder podcasts are essentially . . . Do we have addictive personalities? Are we always just looking for the next rabbit hole we can jump into? Be it podcast, true crime TV show, book, Reddit or subReddit discussion. We're all, in a way, armchair detectives, and the best of detectives are obsessive, aren't they? How else can we explain the explosive growth in popularity of these types of shows?"

"Remember the one show that was going to examine the effects of these cases on the people who obsessively work them, and then they started working the case instead? They became the thing they were supposed to be studying."

"It's easy to do, isn't it?" Nancy says. "Which is why this is such a good reminder to us and all our listeners."

"Part of what we're doing here," Merrick says, "a big part, is consuming other people's tragedies, isn't it? Think about that. How warped is that. We eat darkness. We inject sin. We're bloody voyeurs, virtual rubberneckers but on steroids."

"When you say it like that," Daniel says, "I wonder if there's any redeeming qualities in what we're doing."

"It's redeeming if we help catch a killer," Nancy says. "If we or our audience uncovers hidden evidence that helps the police solve the case."

"But if we don't do that?" he says. "If we only talk about it for a while then go on to something else, which . . . by the way, is what most of these shows do. They all start by saying they're doing it to help solve the crime, but then when they don't, when they've talked in circles long enough, they just start a second season. Maybe add some sponsorships along the way. If that's all we do, what are we good for?"

"Entertainment," Nancy says. "Only. Nothing else. Nothing more. And if that's all it is, we need to find something else to do."

Chapter Forty-two

Anna meets me at my car and hugs me for a long moment. "Are you okay?"

We're in the paved parking lot not far from the wooded walkway that leads to the cottage where Sam and Daniel are staying.

I nod. "Worried about Reggie. Feel guilty for not doing more at the scene, exhausted, need sleep, but . . . I'm okay. And now . . . I'm great. Never been anything but great in your arms."

"Do you feel like doing this?" she asks.

"Don't really feel like we can back out," I say.

"Reggie called. They're not going. And now Daniel says he's not going."

"Why?"

"I'm not sure. Would you talk to him?"

"Of course. I need to make one more call. Could you send him out here?"

"Yeah. Unless . . . well, if we're not going, there's no need to talk him into going, is there?"

"I feel like we have to—even if we're the only ones who do."

"Okay. I'll give you a couple of minutes to make your call then I'll send him out."

We kiss and she departs, returning to the unit where Sam and Daniel are, and where Merrill is with both his Beretta and shotgun.

When I see that she is safely inside, I call Jerry Raffield.

"Finally got some information about the email you received," I say.

"Was it from her?" he asks, his voice desperately hopeful and yet without expectation.

"No. I'm very sorry. It's . . . unbelievable I have to tell you this, but . . . it was from a teenager playing a prank."

"Oh my God," he says, and I can hear in his voice a new low in the level of disappointment he feels in his fellow human beings.

"He and his little brother made the confession video too," I say. "The one that was posted online, on the podcast website. Was trying to see how many views he could get."

"You're kidding. Please tell me this isn't real."

"I'm very sorry."

"The torture and agony never ends, does it?" he says. "How could a kid be so cruel, so . . . depraved?"

"I honestly don't know. I know it has something to do with the anonymous, disconnected, dissociative life online, but . . . that's only part of it."

"Please tell me you can prosecute the parents."

"I wish I had better news for you," I say. "Maybe we will the next time I call. I certainly hope so. Again, I'm sorry."

I end the call as I see Daniel walking this way.

"How's it going?" I ask.

He shakes his head. "Not great. Did Anna ask you to talk to me?"

"We just wondered why you weren't going with us for dinner at Nancy's. I know it would mean a lot to her."

"I'm sorry. I just can't."

"Something with Sam?" I ask. "Don't want to leave her?"

"Something like that."

"Okay," I say, nodding. "I understand. Let us know if we can do anything to help."

"You mean besides all y'all are already doing?"

I smile. "Yeah."

"Okay. Thanks."

He turns to walk back up to the cottage but stops and turns back toward me again.

"Actually, I . . . could really use a . . . Could I talk to you in confidence?"

"Of course."

"I mean the strictest of confidence. I'd die of shame if anyone ever heard this."

"Sure," I say. "What is it?"

"I try not to complain or let on, but . . . this thing with Sam is . . . very hard."

I nod.

"It's . . . it's not the caring for her, helping her, having to do everything for her. That stuff's tough, but . . . nothing compared to . . . how much I miss her."

"I imagine it would be . . . I'm amazed at how well you're handling everything, but know it has to be nearly impossible. I'm glad you're talking to me."

"I miss her so much. Miss what we had. Miss . . . so many things."

I nod again.

"I'm just so lonely. And . . . given what Nancy is going through—something similar . . . I just don't want to even want anybody but Sam—no matter what shape Sam is in. So I'm . . . I've got to be careful how I spend my time, who I spend it with, and where it takes my mind, those dangerous little thoughts that . . . God, I feel so fuckin' guilty. I'm not this man. I'm not."

"What you're experiencing is so natural and normal, you'd be a freak if you didn't feel it," I say. "And you're handling it the exact right way—talking about it, so you can get some understanding and accountability, and removing yourself from any situation that might lead you down a path you don't want to go."

"It's . . . I hope you don't think I've done anything inappropriate. I haven't. But I just feel the need to keep certain relationships professional. Not to be in a social setting or situation."

"We'll bring you some leftovers."

"Don't even want that. Just bring Merrill a plate. See, like with him, with Zaire. She's with him. The way Anna's with you or Reggie's with Merrick. It's just when someone is . . . untethered or . . . like me. You know what I mean. The lack of . . . certain visible boundaries and encumbrances . . . is what I'm finding so challenging—again, just in my mind. But talking has helped. Thank you. And please don't say anything to anyone."

"I won't. And keep talking to me. Let me know any time you're feeling especially vulnerable or tempted. Just call me. Anytime. And I'll check on you from time to time too."

"Thank you, John. Thank you so much."

Chapter Forty-three

"I honestly don't think I'm gonna be able to solve this case," I say.

Anna and I are driving along Highway 98 between Port St. Joe and Apalach, on our way to Nancy's.

"Why?" she asks.

I shake my head. "I'm not sure."

"It's not that it's too cold," she says. "You've solved much older and colder cases than this."

I nod. "No, it's not that. Though that might be part of it. I don't know. I can't decide whether I don't have enough information and evidence or that, because of the media attention, I've been inundated with too many theories."

She seems to think about it.

"It's just a feeling," I say, "but it's persistent."

"You ever felt this way before?"

"Not quite like this," I say. "I always have doubts, always question whether or not I'll be able to close certain cases, but . . . with this one . . . just have an overwhelming feeling that I won't."

"What if you don't?" she asks. "Can you be okay with that?"

I shrug. "Depends on your definition of *okay*," I say with a smile.

"Will you be able to let it go at some point?"

"Probably not completely."

"But I mean have peace, some sense of equilibrium even if you still work on it on an ongoing basis."

"Pretty sure I'll need your help with that," I say.

"What I'm here for," she says, and touches my hand.

Dinner is nice.

Jake joins us, coming inside from where he's been guarding the house.

Nancy is a good cook, and her house, though small and partially a hospital, is immaculate. She doesn't have much, but what she has is nice and well maintained.

The four of us sit at her small dining room table and eat salad, gumbo, and seafood lasagna.

From her position at the table, she is able to check on her husband, Jeff, in the front bedroom across the way, which she does often. The setup and the way she is with him is not dissimilar to the way Daniel is with Sam, and I could see they'd be of great support and comfort to one another.

"This is so good," Anna says.

"It really is," I add.

"This is how she's been feeding me since I've been here," Jake says. "I've put on fifteen pounds already."

"Glad y'all like it, but stop. Y'all are embarrassing me."

Beneath her blond hair and tired blue eyes Nancy's face and neck blush crimson.

"Change of subject," she says. "How is Reggie doing?"

"She's gonna be okay," I say. "Especially since the kid is. But . . . it's tough."

"But so is she," Anna says.

"Yes she is," I agree.

"I really appreciate what you said on the last show I listened to," Anna says to Nancy. "About murder not being entertainment. It was great and really needed to be said."

Nancy gives her a small smile and nod as she looks back toward Jeff. "Think about the kid who got his little brother shot. Posting the video. Sending the email. It's all a game to him. Randa's not a real person. She's a . . . That's the thing that's shocked me the most throughout my entire experience with Jeff and doing my podcast and now the one with the guys. The utter lack of empathy so many people have. I'm sure some are sociopaths with no souls, but most are just so self-involved, so caught up in what they see as this latest form of entertainment . . . they don't get it."

"It's not unlike the way many people treat celebrities," Anna says. "Like they're not real, like they're there for our entertainment—even their personal and private lives."

"Exactly," Nancy says. "That's it. It's exactly like that."

"People," Jake says, shaking his head. "People are dicks."

"I'm glad we did that," Anna says.

We are back in the car, driving home in the dark on 98 along the rim of the bay, a low-slung moon creating a pale path on the undulating water.

"She's got a pretty lonely, claustrophobic life," she adds.

"She did until Jake came along," I say.

She laughs. "Us being there seemed to mean a lot to her."

I nod. "Glad we pressed through and did it. Wish everybody could've come but . . ."

"Why didn't Daniel? You never said."

I tell her. I tell her because she is me and I don't keep anything from her and she doesn't share it with anyone else.

"Poor thing," she says. "You know a good guy like him is eaten up with guilt—just for having a few thoughts and feelings. Hasn't done anything else, right?"

"Right."

"I realize how much you have on you," she says. "I really do. But maybe you could spend a little extra time with him. Maybe we can both go over more."

"Maybe we should've just moved them in with us instead of at Barefoot Cottages," I say.

"I'm thinking maybe we should have."

I was kidding. She was not.

We are quiet a few moments, riding along next to the black body of water, watching the moon dance on the darkness.

"Would it help if you went over the suspects with me?" she asks. "Sort of talk things through."

"Always."

"Lay it on me."

"A stranger or even serial killer could've happened by at just the right moment and taken her," I say. "Then there are the two men who were at the scene—Roger Lamott, who actually spoke to her, and Donald Wynn, the tow-truck driver who says he just stopped and left his card on her car."

"All good possibilities," she says.

"Her boyfriend or fiancé or ex—whatever he was—Josh Douglas. He wasn't where he was supposed to be and I think some of the surveillance footage shows he was following her. And after I interviewed him, he disappeared."

"Very suspicious," she says. "He's got to be your prime suspect."

I shrug. "Of course, it may not have been his shoes on the surveillance footage. It could've been Brenda Young. She could've killed Randa because she took Chelsea Sylvester away from her or because she blames Randa for her death."

"*Damn*. You do have a lot of promising suspects. What about her parents?"

I shake my head. "Don't really suspect them. Especially Jerry. Lynn won't talk to us, which is suspicious, but could really be grief like she claims. If it's a family member it's more likely her crazy old aunt, Scarlett George, or one of her child molester boyfriends. I hope to talk to Scarlett tomorrow."

"Wow. They just keep coming."

"Yeah, and I'm not even mentioning some of the more farfetched possibilities or strange theories that have been floated our way."

"Thank you for sparing me that."

"Finally, there is British Bob and Bert Stewart and their contractors at Windmark Beach," I say. "I still think one or more of them could've been involved and that there's a good chance that Randa is beneath or in one of their foundations out there."

"What about Annie Kathryn Harrison?" she says. "Do you think the same killer killed her *and* Randa?"

"Certainly haven't ruled it out," I say. "There are just enough similarities and differences to make it impossible to come down on one side or the other. It's maddening. Like everything else about this case."

As we near Port St. Joe, I call Jerry to check on him. He's still in shock that someone would send him an email like that as a prank.

When I finish with him, I call Merrick to check on Reggie. Reggie is sleeping and Merrick says she's had an okay evening, considering.

On our way home, we swing by Daniel and Sam's place to check on them and deliver Merrill a huge plate of food. While we're there, I talk to Daniel some more. He seems to be doing better already—

sticking close to Sam, caressing her affectionately as we talk.

Back in the car on our way home, Anna says, "I never quite realized the extent to which you are a pastoral cop. Makes sense. Of course you are. I've just had the chance to observe it more lately I guess. You take an investigative approach to chaplaincy and a pastoral approach to being an investigator. It's very cool to observe."

"Thank you."

"I know it's too much on you to have two jobs," she says. "I was thinking, Taylor's about ready for me to go back to work—at least part-time. Have you thought about which one you'll give up?"

"I've thought about it," I say. "Haven't come up with anything."

"Wonder if there's a way you can keep doing them both on a part-time basis?"

I shrug. "Something will work out. Let's talk about it again when I'm in a better place."

"I'll put it on the list."

"There's a list?"

Chapter Forty-four

The biggest break in the case comes the next morning when a retired couple helping with the search in Panther Swamp discovers human bones.

After another night of not much sleep, I drive down Overstreet to meet Reggie at the site where FDLE crime scene techs and a forensic anthropologist will soon be sifting through what might be Randa's remains.

By the time I arrive, the scene has been cleared of all but two volunteers—the two who found the bones—and a couple of deputies spooling crime scene tape between the trees.

When I park, Reggie walks over to meet me.

"How are you?" I ask.

"Better. Thanks. Good night's sleep helped."

"Good."

"Helps having this to deal with too," she says.

"What *is* this?" I say.

"Come on," she says, "I'll show you."

She leads me back a short ways into the woods, down an embankment, along a trench with a soggy, sandy bottom, and over to the tipped-up root system of an overturned tree.

On the other side of the tree, in a shallow grave, the skull and only a few other bones here and there are visible—but there are enough to see that the entire skeleton is present.

"Take a good look at it, then we'll go talk to the couple who found it."

I nod and continue looking. "We're supposed to believe that eventually, inevitably erosion revealed what's been buried here for nearly twelve years?"

She smiles. "Seen enough?"

"Anything else found? Clothes? Wallet? Keys?"

"Not so far. We're just preserving the scene for FDLE."

I nod. "Okay. Seen enough."

"Follow me."

She leads me back out to the highway and over to the couple who found the remains.

They are fit and spry but pushing eighty, and I wondered if it was a good idea to have them traversing such an uneven and rough terrain.

"This is Clarke and Sue Morgan," Reggie says. "This is my lead investigator, John Jordan."

We shake hands.

"Tell him what you told me," Reggie says.

"It wasn't there yesterday," Sue says, tucking her gray hair behind her ear with swollen and misshapen fingers.

"What wasn't?" I ask.

"The body," Clarke says.

"The remains," she corrects. "Those bones, that skeleton wasn't there yesterday. We walked right past that fallen tree. Searched both sides thoroughly."

"You're absolutely positive?" I say. "It's a big swamp and a lot of it looks just like the rest of it."

"We're hikers," Sue says. "We have a good sense of forests and swamps. Plus, if you'll look on that overturned tree you'll see a little mark I made—M for Morgan with the date and time. We were there yesterday. We had to walk across yesterday's grid to get to today's."

I nod. "Y'all see anybody else out here, in this grid yesterday or this morning—going or coming— anything that looked suspicious at all?"

They both shake their heads. "Sorry."

"Don't be. Y'all did great. Thank you."

"Bear with me for a few more minutes," Reggie says, "then we'll get you out of here. Okay?"

"We're in no hurry, love," Sue says.

Reggie and I walk back over to my car.

"So?" she says.

"So someone moved those bones from where they were and partially buried them where they are now so they'd be found today—or soon. He had to know the search was taking place in this area. There are signs."

"Why move the remains?"

"Well, if it's her," I say, "if it's Randa . . . to get them off his property—especially if he thinks we're getting close."

"But we're not, are we?"

I shake my head. "If we are, I don't know it. But maybe something we've done—like questioning

him or something . . . has him thinking the net is closing."

"Who's most likely for it to be?"

I shrug. "This happened after the boyfriend disappeared. He's certainly acting suspicious."

"And he was following her," she says.

"Looks like it. But we should also see if there
has been any concrete at Windmark Beach busted up
and/or repoured."

"I'll get somebody over there."

"And Roger Lamott is acting all kinds of nervous and hostile."

"What if after all this time and all these theories
and after looking so far and wide, the only witness we
have from that night is who took her?"

"Has a higher likelihood than about anything
else we're considering."

"Look, we're not gonna know anything from
this for a while," she says. "And even when we do, we
may not know much. FDLE tech on the phone said
best case is the remains can tell us sex, race, and ap-
proximate age. Maybe we'll get lucky and find her wallet or clothes or something."

"But even if you do," I say, "since the remains
were moved, the only things that'll be present are what
whoever moved her wants you to see."

"True. So you find the old couple as credible as
I do?"

I nod. "I assume you're going to check her
mark on the tree."

She nods. "It's there. But back to the . . . remains. Even if we get all that, and even if we find out somehow for sure that it's Randa, that's not gonna tell us who killed her and hid her body out here. So keep working the case. Keep tracking down leads. This could easily become a distraction if we let it."

I nod.

"Work the case so that when we have confirmation it's her, we can make an arrest."

When I get back in my car and check my emails on my phone, I see that I have another from Cold-BloodedKiller@gmail.com.

How many times has somebody gotten the better of you, John? How many unsolved cases haunt you? Bet there haven't been many that you didn't close, right? Surely I won't be the first, but, as I said, I truly doubt you have many. But, make no mistake, you are about to have another. See, here's the difference in us. I'm sure you're familiar with the old Nietzsche quotes. "Beware that, when fighting monsters, you yourself do not become a monster" and "for when you gaze long into the abyss, the abyss gazes also into you." That's the difference. You fight monsters. I am a monster. You gaze into the abyss. I am the abyss. Of course, I'll beat you. How could I not. You're merely trying to capture a thing. I am the thing. Don't feel bad. Did you know that the rate of closed homicide investigations has been going steadily down for decades now? Do you know why that is? Because of monsters like me? Because of the rise of stranger killers? Hey, your rate is much, much higher than the national av-

erage. It's about to be a little worse after me, but it's still way up there. Hold your head up, John. You have nothing to be ashamed of. It's like my mama used to tell me, there's always somebody bigger, faster, stronger, smarter, better. You just ran into someone who is. I'm gonna miss these little talks, John. I truly am.

Chapter Forty-five

After leaving the crime scene, I continue down Overstreet intending to take a left on 98 and head to Windmark to look around.

I know Reggie is going to send someone out to have a look, but I want to see it for myself.

I also plan to talk to British Bob and Bert, but I never got the chance to do any of it.

Before reaching 98, I got a call from a secretary at Gulf Coast State College who I'd asked to keep an eye out for Josh for me.

"He's here now," she says. "Trying to cash in his retirement. He won't be long. You better hurry."

"Don't let him leave. I'm on my way."

"I can't stop him."

"Make up more paperwork or something. Just keep him there."

I put my emergency light on and race through Tyndall Air Force Base and Panama City, and reach the college campus faster than should have been possible.

When I rush into the Employee Financial Services office, Josh is there, impatiently waiting for the secretary to find just one more form she needs him to sign.

"I know it's here somewhere," she says.

When they become aware of me, she glances up quickly and says, "I'll be with you in just a minute, sir," as if she has no idea who I am or why I'm here.

She's good. Scary good.

"Actually," I say, flashing my badge, "I'm here to see him."

"Now's not a good time," he says. "Sorry."

"The time is not in question," I say. "Only the where and the how."

"I don't—"

"You can talk to me here or I can cuff you, lead you across campus to my car, then drive you down to my office for questioning. Up to you."

"Here," he says. "Of course. You don't have to be such an ass."

"Ma'am, do you have a small room we can use?"

Having completely abandoned her search for the important paper for Josh to sign, she stands and leads us over to a small meeting room and closes the door.

"Where have you been?" I say. "Why'd you disappear so abruptly?"

"My dad had a stroke," he says.

"I'm very sorry to hear that. How is he?"

"Not good. Gonna require constant care."

"Where is he?"

"Mobile. Where we've been. Where we're moving. My brother's very wealthy. He's hiring us—my wife and I—to live with and care for Dad. It's a great opportunity because I can . . . it will afford me the chance to finish my book."

"I'll need some names and numbers to verify all this," I say. "When you vanished so thoroughly, I thought—"

"I didn't vanish—thoroughly or otherwise. We went to take care of my dad. It turned into a long-term thing. The truth is . . . I went there thinking and hoping it would. I don't really like teaching at this level. You thought what? What did you think?"

"That you were running because of our new investigation into what happened to Randa."

"What? Wait. *What*? Why would I—oh, you think I . . ."

"We know you were following her," I say. "Surveillance footage shows you—"

"I loved her. Cared for her so . . . deeply. I was decent to her. Something not many people were. I didn't . . . I didn't do anything to her. I didn't even . . . Don't you see? I stopped too soon. I wish I would've kept following her, but I didn't. I gave up. It took a while, but I realized if I stayed with her or tried to—or even someone like her—I'd always be following, always be wondering, always be suspicious. It took me a little while, but that night changed my life. Changed me. I chose that night what sort of man I was going to be and what kind of wife I'd have and . . . I . . . I did it. I became that man. I married that woman. I wouldn't change who I became—except to save Randa. If I had kept following her . . . maybe I could've kept her from getting killed."

"So you followed her all the way to Panama City, then turned around and drove home?"

"No. I called a buddy of mine who lives here and we went drinking. He'll tell you. I'm sure we can scrounge up a few other witnesses too. But it'd be a complete and utter waste of time."

"You mean like what I'm doing here when you could've told authorities this twelve years ago?"

"I . . . I kept waiting for a call or a visit. I didn't try to hide. I figured someone saw me—or some camera picked me up."

"You were hiding from Randa."

"Just to see what she was doing. It was so bizarre—even for her. She didn't usually go off like that—not that far and not by herself. I wanted to see where she was going. Until I didn't. Until I decided not to live my life that way for another second. Give me a polygraph. Verify everything I've told you with witnesses. I have nothing to hide. I just hate for you to waste all your time on me when I know I'm innocent."

"It's good of you to be worried about my time," I say. "Especially when all this would've been easier to verify over a decade ago when it happened."

I toss him my pad and a pen. "Write it all down. Full names. Numbers if you have them. Where your dad is staying. His doctor. Everything."

"Sure," he says, and starts scrawling the information on the paper, "but I told you who you should talk to."

I shake my head. "No. No you didn't."

"I'm sure I did. I always tell everybody."

"Who? Who should I talk to?"

"Randa's aunt. The crazy one. Scarlett George. If she didn't have something to do with this somehow . . . then it was some random serial killer or something, 'cause I don't know who else could be involved. And I know she was trying to reach her aunt in the week after Chelsea died, leading up to her own disappearance."

Chapter Forty-six

"Look at this place," Scarlett George is saying with an outstretched hand. "Look at it."

I did.

"It's a dump."

She's right. It is.

She lives in a small dilapidated duplex off 11th Street in St. Andrews. Literally crumbling down around her, the structure doesn't look particularly safe to be in.

There is very little furniture—and what there is, is filthy and covered with piles of laundry.

"Think about all that money they have," she says, "and look at this place."

I shake my head. "It's unbelievable. Some people can be so selfish it borders on the cruel."

She likes the sound of that, nodding as she squints her eyes. I can tell she's trying it on for size, and will use it with them or someone about them someday soon. "Borders on the cruel," she repeats.

She is slumped in a high-back chair in the middle of the small living room, a muted TV balancing precariously on a folding chair in front of her.

Her hair is unkempt, and though she used to keep it dyed scarlet, it now appears there's a rust-colored little fox on her head. Her clothes are wrinkled—and don't match. And she looks at least a decade older than she is.

"It really does."

"I'm not saying I didn't have my differences with that child," she says. "She was another one more selfish than you can imagine, but . . . you can't convince me she'd want her poor aunt to be living like this when she left so much money behind for us."

Scarlett George is a sad person, a drug-fried, low-IQ narcissist who is actually on a partial high at the moment.

And I'm going to do my best to take advantage of that.

"She'd want you to have it," I say. "To take care of yourself. To live in a better place. To have a better life."

She nods. "To have a better life. Exactly. She knew how much I suffered, how hard I've had it. You can't tell me even a self-centered only child like her wouldn't want to help her own flesh and blood if she could."

"And she can," I say.

She nods. "If they would let her."

"Maybe we can make them."

She sits up and draws her head back. "Really? How so?"

"I think you may have some legal remedies," I say. "My wife's an attorney."

"Shame you're married."

"But what might work even faster is a visit from a guy with a gun and a badge."

She smiles a gleefully sick smile, her hooded eyes opening at the prospects of being able to throw a cop at her troubles.

"Nothing makes me happier than knocking down high and mighty bitches think they're better than everybody else," I say, "think they can just keep all the money for themselves."

"It's just him," she says. "I know it is. He's stoppin' her somehow. She's always helped out at least a little over the years. Not nearly what she could . . . but always something. Now . . . it's gotta be him that's keeping her from it."

"You're talkin' about Jerry, right?"

"Yeah. *Jerry.*"

I open my eyes wide as if something just occured to me. "Wait a minute," I say.

"What? What is it?"

"I may have an even better idea," I say. "One that will get you the money a lot faster and not require any rough stuff."

"Oh yeah? What's that?"

"They have that money put up for a reward."

"So they say."

"You help me a little and I'll see what I can do about getting them to give you the reward. You'll have earned it fair and square. Nobody can say anything."

"People always say stuff, but . . . I get what you mean. And I do have some information."

"I know you do," I say. "That's what makes it so perfect."

"How do you know I—"

"I know Randa called you the day she disappeared," I say.

Actually, what I knew was that Randa had been trying to reach her the week after Chelsea died and before Randa disappeared. I was guessing that she eventually got through to Scarlett.

"It was the day before," she says. "Well, the night before. She called all upset. She had been calling. Calling and calling. She could be relentless when she wanted to be. I finally answered just to get her to stop. She was a blithering mess. A friend of hers had died. It was her fault. Except it wasn't her fault. It was my fault."

"Your fault?" I say. "Why would she say that?"

"Kid's always had a vivid imagination," she says. "Figured she'd grow up to be an actress or some kind of strange artist or something. Said my Bill touched her when she was little and that she never got over it and that's why she is the way she is and yada yada yada. Boohoo. What kid ain't been touched? Ain't no big deal. I can tell you I never blamed the little diddlin' I got as a kid on any of the bad shit that's ever happened to me. Never used it for an excuse."

"What did she use it as an excuse for?" I ask.

She shrugs. "I don't know. Like that has anything to do with bein' able to keep a man or not. Said some crazy shit."

"Like?"

"Like sex stuff. Addiction bullshit. You either like sex or you don't, right? And most everybody do, don't they? Ain't no *addicted to* bullshit. She was talking crazy. Like I said, she . . . was always high-strung. Ain't sayin' that's what got her killed, but . . . wouldn't surprise me none, I can tell you that."

"But surely she didn't just call to tell you all that shit," I say. "Just to bitch at you and blame you for her actions."

"Only one person she blamed more than me," she says. "And by God she meant to have it out with him. Sounded like she wouldn't be happy 'til she killed him."

"Bill?" I say.

She looks up at me and nods. "He went by Bill Lee a lot. Thought it was cute 'cause his name was Billy. He wasn't cute. Just thought he was. He was a mean bastard. Nasty. Liked to hurt people. Full name was Billy LaDuke."

"And she wanted to know where he was?" I ask. "Wanted to take out her rage for how she was and her friend's death on him?"

"Yeah."

"What'd you tell her?"

"Told her she was a silly little girl who didn't want nothing to do with that mean man. I've known some cruel bastards in my time. Felt their bite. But Billy . . . he's the . . . he makes all the rest look like child's play."

"Did she get it out of you?" I ask. "Did you tell her where he was?"

"Didn't know it to tell. Told her last I ever knew of him he was working construction in St. Joe, but that had been a while. No idea where he was then or now."

"That's what she was doing out there," I say. "She was on her way to Port St. Joe to confront the monster who was still haunting her life."

"Then she's a bigger fool than even I thought."

My mind runs ahead of me. In an instant I see Randa running into Windmark where Billy LaDuke is working, yelling all manner of accusations at him, beginning to hit and kick him. Is he there alone? Was it his van Bert noticed? He lashes out. Punches her in the face. Picks up a framing hammer and finishes the job. Then buries her beneath the foundation a few hours before it's poured. Then to put more distance between where he used to work and where her body is found he digs her up and moves her across the street into the swamp.

Maybe none of it happened that way, but the movie in my mind is vivid, graphic, disturbing, and most troubling of all, it fits with the facts.

Of course, the facts can be fit together in other ways too. In a less sleep-deprived state I could come up with a few of them.

"Did she say anything else?" I ask. "Tell you she was headed to Port St. Joe to exact her revenge?"

"She said all kinds of jibber jabber mish mash."

"Did you try to stop her? Tell her parents? The police? Anybody?"

"I got better things to do than get involved with some silly young girl's dramatic bullshit."

Chapter Forty-seven

"She was on her way to Port St. Joe to find the man who raped her as a child," I say to Reggie. "Still can't account for the eight-hour gap during the day but I am pretty sure about this."

I'm racing through Panama City with my emergency lights flashing and my siren on.

"That's what she was doing where she was," I say. "Losing her friend really got to her. She blamed herself. Which meant she really blamed her step-uncle or whatever he was—the pederast with her drug-addicted, narcissistic aunt at the time. We've got to find him."

"You think he killed her when she came looking for him?"

"I think it's a good possibility," I say.

"What's his name?"

"Billy LaDuke," I say.

"I'll find him. How far out are you?"

"Forty-five minutes. Be there as fast as I can. What's the word on the remains?"

"FDLE just left," she says. "Tech told me the skeleton is definitely female and around the right age. So it could be her."

"They confirm she had been moved recently?"

"Yeah. Say they may be able to give us a good idea from where after they get everything back to the lab and test it."

"Cool."

"We're getting there, John," she says. "We're gonna close this thing. After twelve years."

And until she said that I guess some part of me actually thought we might, but the moment I heard her verbalize it, to actually make her hopeful declaration, I knew we wouldn't, knew somehow we were already too late.

A few moments after ending my call with Reggie, my phone starts vibrating again. The call is coming from an undisclosed number.

"John Jordan," I say as I answer it.

"Hello, Mr. Chaplain Detective John Jordan," a digitally demented voice says.

Instantly I know it's him.

"What should I call you?" I ask.

"By my actual name," he says. "Jeffrey Dixon Hunter. That's my real name and this is an actual confession. Every single word of it is true. I'm not some punk kids playing a prank. I sent your friends the real picture of Randa and I've been emailing you. I'm telling you everything because it's too late for you to do anything about it. Understand?"

"I understand."

"Were you able to track me through my emails or the Snapchat image I sent?"

"No."

"And you won't be able to trace this call or track me now, but feel free to try if you must. But whatever you do, listen to me carefully. You need to really pay attention to what I'm saying. Okay?"

"I'm listening."

"I'm a cold-blooded killer. It's just the way I'm wired. You might call me sick. And maybe I am. But I love to have my way with young women—and my way is hurtin' 'em with my hands and my dick. Preferably at the same time. Y'all got it wrong. That little black girl . . . she wasn't killed by her brother's loser drug suppliers. I crushed that sweet little grape. God, was she good. So tight and strong. Love the ones with endurance . . . ones that like to tussle."

He pauses but I don't say anything.

"Am I shocking you?" he asks.

"I only wish you were."

"Heard a few confessions over the years, have you? Still, can't be easy."

"Honestly," I say, "it's a lot easier hearing a straight confession or even someone bragging about what he's done than it is someone making excuses and justifications and blaming the victims or their parents or the TV."

"There is no excuse for what I do," he says. "No justification for rape and murder. And that's exactly what it is. Rape. I rape women. I hurt them. I brutalize them. I overpower them and do just what I want to with them. And I murder women. When I'm done fuckin' them I snuff them out. Doesn't even take much effort."

He pauses but I don't say anything, just think of a world where there are men like Jeffrey Dixon Hunter, the same world Anna and my little girls inhabit, and I'm filled with such rage I want to beat such men to death with my bare fists.

"Early on I told you I'd beat you, didn't I?" he says.

"You did."

"And I have. I'm only telling you the things I'm telling you because I'm already gone and you'll never find me. You lose. You were no match for me. I'm not saying you wouldn't have found me eventually. I was right there in front of you, after all, but . . . you didn't find me or grab me when you had the chance. I won."

"What happened to Randa?" I ask.

"Acknowledge I beat you first, then I'll tell you."

"You beat me," I say. "Clearly."

"Do you even know why Randa was where she was yet?"

"I think so. Looking for someone from her past."

"John, that makes him sound like a former lover or a coach from high school. She was looking for the monster who ruined her life. And she ran into another one. A worse one. She was all hopped up on pills, booze, and revenge. Slid her little car around on the road. And here's the important part of that. She hit her head. *Thwack*. Forehead to steering wheel. Check. See . . . all you investigators and all those armchair detectives with their silly little podcasts . . . y'all all thought the odds of someone like me coming along in the seven minutes or so she was out there alone were just too great. I mean, *fuck*, what would odds like that even be? But it wasn't exactly like that. No, our little dazed and confused girl wandered around for a while. Got away from her car. Started walking. Hid from the tow truck and the cop and anyone else who passed by. But eventually came upon me."

He pauses again and I wait.

"I know you have questions," he says. "I know you want more details. I left it all behind for you. It's there. You'll find it. I've got no problem with you looking, with you digging up the rest of the info. What I would have a problem with is you coming after me. That's a no-no. And I've taken out a little insurance policy to make sure you don't. So please don't be stupid. Don't come after me and I'll guarantee a happy ending for you and the rest of them. Come after me and I guarantee not only will you never find me but you'll never see one of your friends again. Listen to me, John. Are you listening? Everything I've told you is true. All this really happened. But pretty soon you're gonna get some more information that will—that should greatly impact your decision. Listen to it. Let it in. Go against your instincts. Save your friend. Prepare yourself to do that now so that when the time comes you'll be ready. That's what this little call was about. To try to get you prepared. To say I beat you. And to say goodbye and that it's been a real pleasure watching you work this thing. It really has. Now let it go and get yourself some rest. You need it."

Chapter Forty-eight

"Are y'all okay?" I ask.

As soon as the killer disconnects the call, I phone Anna.

"Yes. Why? What's wrong?"

"Dad and Verna are there with you, right? And you can see Taylor?"

"I'm holding her and yes they are. Why?"

"Just a new threat from the killer," I say. "Tell dad to keep his weapon drawn and ready for the next little while until I call back. Y'all stay inside and keep the doors locked. Would you call Frank Morgan and tell him to do the same for Johanna?"

"I will and we will, but you're the one who needs to be careful. Who's guarding you? You're out there with him."

"I'll be extra careful," I say. "Call you in just a little while. Love you."

"Love you."

As soon as I end the call with Anna, I call Reggie.

"I was just about to call you," she says.

"Before we do anything else," I say, "we need to take a roll call. I just had a call from the killer and he's threatening one of us. Will you check on Merrick and your kids? I'll check in with Jake and Merrill about

Sam, Daniel, and Nancy. Tell everyone to stay put and be vigilant until we get a better sense of what's going on."

Without waiting for a response, I end the call, tap in Merrill's number, and tell him what's going on.

"Everything quiet here," he says. "They not even up yet."

"Double check," I say. "Wake them up if you have to. I'm gonna call Jake. I'll call you back when I can."

Two more taps and Jake's line is ringing.

After several rings and no answer it goes to voicemail.

I leave him a message and then call him right back.

Same thing again. Several rings. No answer. Voicemail.

And again.

And again.

As I'm coming into town and trying Jake yet again, my phone begins to vibrate. It's Merrill.

"He's not here," he says.

"Who?"

"Daniel. He's gone. I've searched the whole house. There's no sign of forcible entry and I would've heard it if there was. His car is still parked out in the lot. His wallet and keys are still in his bedroom. But he's gone. Guess he could be out on the property for some reason—walking, checking the mail, hell, I don't know, but I can't watch her and go out looking for him."

"Stay with her," I say. "I'll send a deputy over to search the grounds."

"Can't fuckin' believe I lost him, man. *Shee-it.* Ain't like me."

"We'll find him," I say, and hang up.

A moment later Reggie is calling.

"Merrick and all our kids are good and to-gether," she says. "And I have a deputy out in front of the house. And before I forget—nobody reported Billy LaDuke missing, but he's been missing a very long time now. He used to live in a camper or van or something on the sites where he worked. The people he was working for just thought he took off—the way contractors do. Wonder if he took Randa and van-ished or . . . Where are you?"

"Coming into town. Daniel is missing. Merrill is inside keeping an eye on Sam. Can you send a deputy over to Barefoot Cottages to search the grounds for Daniel—preferably someone who knows him?"

"Done," she says. "I'll—"

"And Jake's not answering. Can you call the Franklin County Sheriff's Department and get some-one over to Nancy's place to check on them?"

"On it. Call you right back."

When she is gone, I call Merrick.

"Hey, Reggie told me what's going on," he says. "You okay?"

"Having trouble reaching Jake and I don't have Nancy's number. Can you call her and check on them?"

"I've tried her a few times this morning and keep getting her voicemail, but I'll keep trying."

"Let me know when you get her," I say. "And text me her number just so I'll have it."

When I end the call with him, I try Jake again. And again I get his voicemail.

I disconnect and call him again.

And this time I get him.

"John?" he says in a confused and groggy voice. "You . . . gotta . . . see . . . this. Get down here . . . fast as you can."

I see Reggie up ahead, not far from the Sunset Coastal Grill. Her vehicle is parked on the side of the road, its emergency lights on.

I pull in behind her and she jumps into the car with me.

"Franklin County deputy at the house says it's an active crime scene and there's a letter addressed to you. Let's go."

Chapter Forty-nine

The first thing I notice when we pull into Nancy's small yard is that Jake is okay. He's standing in a small group of deputies running his mouth—something I've never been so glad to see him do.

I hug him when I walk up.

He looks a little embarrassed to be hugged by another man in front of the Franklin County deputies, but gives in and gives me a quick hug back.

"You okay?"

"Just a little loopy," he says.

"More so than usual?" I ask.

"I was drugged," he says. "Was out all night and most of the day. I'm fine. You need to get in there and . . ."

I catch up with Reggie near the front of the house, and the Franklin County sheriff, a tall middle-aged man with a potbelly, gives us gloves and leads us in.

The house is empty except for Nancy's husband Jeff on his hospital bed in the front bedroom.

"Jake said a woman lives here too," the sheriff says. "No sign of her."

We walk into the front bedroom after him.

A young female paramedic in navy pants and a white uniform shirt is monitoring his vitals. "He's stable," she says. "Just sleeping."

"Thanks, Margaret. Could you excuse us a minute?"

"Sure, Sheriff."

She leaves.

On the hospital table next to Jeff's bed is a sealed envelope with my name on it.

"Why don't you take a look at that while I bring Sheriff Varney up to speed on what we're dealing with?" Reggie says.

I nod, reaching for the envelope with my gloved hand while she tells the older man about the Randa Raffield case.

Dear John,

I only realized how that sounds after I wrote it, but it fits. Because this is a breakup letter of sorts. It's funny, but I really will miss you. Miss this. Miss everyone. Well, almost everyone. Every word I confessed to you on the phone as Jeffrey this morning was true. It just wasn't my confession to make. It was this man's, the one in the hospital bed—Jeffrey Dixon Hunter. And he was a hunter. A mean, vicious, prick of a predator. He attacked me like I told you. It happened just like that. I was there to confront Billy LaDuke. That's all. Had no intention of killing him. Just had to face down the monster, which I did. When I realized that the place where I had my little accident was in walking distance from his construction site, I locked my car, hid for a while, and then walked over there. I knew he slept in a van or a camper on site, but when I got there he was still working. I told him how fucked up I was because of what he had done to me, how much I was hurting others, and how that meant he was still hurting others. I tried to tell him, to share my truth with him, but he went crazy. Started yelling and shaking. And then he hit me. Just punched me hard in the face. Knocked me down. I jumped up. Fought back. But I was no match. Hunter stepped in. I thought he was saving me. He and Billy fought. And he killed him. But he wasn't saving me. Well, he was, but for himself. He wanted me for his own sick, twisted pleasure. LaDuke is buried under British Bob's house in Windmark Beach subdivision. Hunter buried him there then pounced on me. He beat me and raped me there but then brought me back to this place and did all kinds of other shit to me. Told me he had just buried Annie Kathryn Harrison in the backyard and I'd soon be in the hole with her. But he underestimated me and my resolve to change myself and my life. When he thought he had beaten me too bloodied and blue to do anything but take more of his worst, I got his knife while he was coming in me for the third time that first night and I used it to turn the tables. I couldn't save Annie Kathryn, but I could save myself and many other future victims. I could work on changing myself and my life while I made his a living hell. It takes a special strength and discipline, commitment and cold-bloodedness to do what I did, to keep doing it for as long as I have. It's why I knew you wouldn't beat me. Why I knew no one would. I used not to be, but I am now the strongest person I know, the strongest I have ever known. I am a victim no more. Speaking of you not beating me . . . Sorry for the braggadocios emails. I was trying to sound like LaDuke or Hunter would. Oh, and by the way, the picture I sent Daniel and Merrick was real. Hunter took it while he was doing what he did to me. Anyway, I'm not a killer, but I have become cold blooded. I was made, not born. It hasn't been easy. The hardest part was not telling my dad I was okay. I started to several times, but in time even that got easier. So this is what I did. I hobbled Hunter, immobilized him for good, and began drugging him—heavily when people were around, lighter when it was just us and I wanted to make sure he remembered what was happening to him and why and who was behind it. I won't get into all the details of what I did, but an incredible transformation took place in this little house. It's not inaccurate to say that Jeffrey Dixon Hunter killed Randa Raffield. He did. What was left of her. What he did and how I responded gave birth to Nancy Drury, the smartest, baddest bitch I know. I've had a few friends and lovers over the years—people who felt sorry for the widow whose hit-and-run husband was such a burden. I've spent years studying criminal psychology, homicide investigation, missing persons investigation. You name it. Became obsessed with catching evil fuckers like LaDuke and Hunter. And a few years ago I began to do these podcasts about true crime and criminals and I got pretty good at catching them, at helping take them down in one way or another. That's also how I knew you were good, but I was better. So everything's going along all nice and fine until some of these little armchair detectives want to solve my case, want to know what happened to me. I listened. I watched. I read. And eventually, I joined the team, I became part of the investigation, the podcast, the phenomenon that was the search for me. I already had the dyed-blond hair and blue contacts. I had already put on a little weight, had already been keeping a little sun on my face, and hell, I had aged over a decade. I was set. I knew I'd have to move along eventually, but until then I'd keep up with the investigation and make all the plans and preparations so that you nor anyone else would ever be able to find me. Not ever. But just to make sure you don't, I took a little insurance. The nicest, sweetest, gentlest man among y'all, Daniel. So, John, here's my deal. I just want to be left alone. That's it. I haven't killed anybody. I'm not a murderer. So why not just leave me alone? You really think the false imprisonment of a rapist and murderer like Hunter is worth coming after me for? Really? If y'all will leave me be, not come after me, I'll not only take good care of Daniel but I'll return him to you safe and unharmed very soon. Providing, of course, he wants to return home. By then, who knows. He's pretty smitten with me. Oh, and tell your friend, the big black guy, not to waste time feeling bad. Daniel snuck out to meet me. I told him I had to talk to him privately and I needed to do it right then. He climbed out of the master bathroom window. Your friend did nothing wrong. Except maybe underestimate me. Y'all've all done that. Just like everybody else in my life. Do we have a deal, John? Will you take the defeat graciously and leave me and Daniel alone? If you do you get him back. Oh, and just know this—I left fairly early last night. I'm already where I'm going and I can't be traced or tracked or found or extradited. So all you'll do by trying is to cause poor Sam's life to get even worse than it already is—which, as I understand it, is because of you to begin with, right? Whatta you say? Have you done enough damage to this couple? Will you let your bruised ego at getting beat by a girl get the better of you, or will you let Daniel live? We shall soon see.

Bye for now (or is it forever?),
Me

Chapter Fifty

Though the letter had been written to me, how to respond to it isn't my decision. Within seconds of reading it, Sheriff Varney orders roadblocks in Franklin County and Reggie does the same in Gulf. BOLOs are issued. Searches begun.

It's all pointless. Randa is long gone. And Daniel with her.

She has a fourteen-hour head start. She could be in Cuba. Or Texas or Tennessee. And if they flew, they could be on the other side of the world.

"She's wrong about your ego, isn't she?" Reggie says.

It's much later and we are driving back toward Gulf County together.

"Huh?" I say, rousing out of thought.

I can tell I'm in shock, a dissonant distance between my thoughts and my ability to process them. Disbelief that Daniel is gone.

"You don't mind the fact that it was a woman who pulled this off," she says. "No more than a man. She put in her letter that part about you being beaten by a girl."

"Oh," I say. "No. And I don't look at it in terms of winning and losing. It's not a game to me. I don't mind that she beat me. To be honest, if she truly

293

hasn't killed anyone, even with what she did to Hunter—given who he is and what he did to her and Annie Kathryn, I wouldn't have minded her just disappearing. Wouldn't have even felt the need to look for her all that hard. What I mind is that I failed Daniel. That's . . . the . . ."

"You were lead investigator, sure, but we were all working the case. We all failed to find her in time—though you were getting close. You had found the scent. She knew her days were numbered. The failure to protect Daniel is on all of us. But . . . he snuck out. That's not exactly our failure to protect. Can't protect someone who doesn't want to be. Why would he do that? It didn't seem odd to him that she was asking him to crawl through his window to—"

"He just thought they were keeping their meeting a secret," I say. "He thought they were just two lonely people with incapacitated spouses who were—"

"Oh," she says. "*Oh.*"

"He had no idea what he was walking into."

"Poor Daniel. Poor Sam. What will happen to her now?"

"Anna and I've talked. We're gonna move her in with us. Until we get Daniel back or she's able to live on her own again."

"John, that's . . . it's incredible of you guys, but . . . the chances of either of those things happening are . . . so . . . slim. You sure you know what you're signing up for?"

"We do."

"You feel responsible for what happened to both of them," she says. "But you're not. You're not."

I don't say anything and we ride along in silence for a while.

Up ahead on the highway near the county line, cars are lined up at the roadblock.

"You think we were wrong to set up the road-blocks?" she asks.

"I think she's long gone—and was before the sun came up this morning."

"You think she'll kill him?"

"Not because of roadblocks. I . . . I don't think she will. I think she likes Daniel. So far as we know she hasn't killed anyone."

"What she did to Jeffrey Dixon Hunter was worse than death," she says. "Think about what she's done to him and for how long."

"It shows a metal at her core like I've rarely en-countered," I say. "Maybe never. She's . . . one of the strongest, smartest, most capable people I've ever en-countered."

"You *admire* her?" she asks in surprise. "Tell me she's not capable of murder."

"The things she said on the podcast—I think she meant them. I think she has a highly developed sense of justice. I think she cares deeply about victims, that she's outraged at the wickedness and brutality of criminal depravity inflicted on innocent and unsus-pecting victims. I'm not saying she won't do whatever she feels she has to to survive, but I don't think she'll kill Daniel."

"I hope you're right," she says. "You have a higher opinion of her than I do."

"Merrick spent a lot of time with her," I say. "See what he thinks."

"Already have," she says. "He shares your opinion."

"We could both be delusional," I say. "In denial that Daniel could already be dead—or that he might be soon."

Chapter Fifty-one

"You okay?" Anna asks.

She has just come up behind me on our back patio where I am standing and thinking and looking at the last of the light over Lake Julia.

It's the middle of October, and the evening is cool, the quality of its light stark. Just behind the pines and cypress trees along the far side of Julia, a low jack-o-lantern-orange glow is fading into nothingness.

"Is it okay if I'm not?" I ask.

"Of course," she says. "Just don't expect me not to try to make it better."

It's been two weeks and no word from Daniel. He is now as missing as any one of the poor vanished young women most of the true crime podcasts are about.

Through the French doors behind us, Sam's hospital bed is set up in the center of our living room and she's sleeping peacefully in it. In a few moments, Merrill and Zaire will arrive for dinner, followed a little later by Dad and Verna and Reggie and Merrick.

But I don't feel like company, have no appetite for food or companionship.

How can I enjoy a meal or the warmth of my friends while Daniel is still out there somewhere, a soul in purgatory, a light, like the one behind the lake before me, going out.

Out, out, brief candle! Life's but a walking shadow . . .

A random snippet of Shakespeare surfaces, but I stifle any more.

"What can I do?" Anna asks.

I shrug. "You're doing it. You're doing all you can do. Thanks for all you're doing. I'm sorry I'm . . . It's just hard to . . . I feel so . . . I'll get better."

"And sooner or later we'll find him," she says. "Or she'll return him."

I try to nod, but can't quite do it.

"Thank you," I say.

"For what?"

"Well, everything. You're such a generous, incredible partner, but just then I was appreciating you understanding how I feel and not telling me to get over it, to suck it up buttercup."

She laughs. "I'd never say *suck it up buttercup.*"

"And thank you for that too."

"Let me tell you something, John Jordan," she says. "I believe in you like I've never believed in anyone. Ever. If I were out there somewhere, you're who I'd want looking for me. So you do what you've got to do—grieve, process, figure it out—whatever it is, and then you find Daniel for us."

"'M I interrupting?" Merrill asks as he joins us on the back porch.

"Never," Anna says, turning and hugging him.

When she lets go of him, he actually steps over and gives me a hug too.

Our hug has an economy and brevity his and hers did not. When he pulls back—something he starts doing the moment the hug begins—he narrows his eyes and nods at me.

"I figure in addition to whatever else you doin', you lookin' for the professor," he says to me.

I nod.

"I'm in," he says. "I lost him. I should help find him."

"You certainly should," I say, nodding vigorously.

"Way I figure it . . . between the four of us—Zaire in on this too—we oughta have Daniel back least by the time Sam firin' on all eight cylinders again."

"Helps to have a deadline," Anna says.

"I is goal oriented," he says, a broad smile spreading across his face.

"Let's go eat and discuss how we're gonna do it," Anna says.

They turn and head in, but I linger behind and take one more look at Julia.

Standing there, staring into the gloom, I wonder where Daniel is at this moment. Is he scared? Suffering one of his panic attacks? Is he drugged? Conscious? Aware? Does he know we're coming for him? That we won't stop until we find him?

Surely he does. Surely if he knows anything, he knows that.

About the Author

Michael grew up in North Florida near the Gulf of Mexico and the Apalachicola River in a small town world famous for tupelo honey.

Truly a regional writer, North Florida is his beat.

Captivated by story since childhood, Michael has a love for language and narrative inspired by the Southern storytelling tradition that captured his imagination and became such a source of meaning and inspiration. He holds undergraduate and graduate degrees in theology with an emphasis on myth and narrative.

In the early 90s, Michael became the youngest chaplain within the Florida Department of Corrections. For nearly a decade, he served as a contract, staff, then senior chaplain at three different facilities in the Panhandle of Florida—a unique experience that led to his first novel, 1997's critically acclaimed, **POWER IN THE BLOOD**. Michael's books take readers through the electronically locked gates of the chain-link fences, beneath the looping razor wire glinting in the sun, and into the strange world of Potter Correctional Institution, Florida's toughest maximum security prison.

Michael lives with his wife Dawn in Wewahitchka, FL.

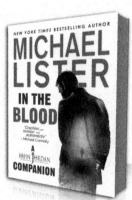

CPSIA information can be obtained
at www.ICGtesting.com
Printed in the USA
BVOW03*0941271017
498751BV00013B/8/P